Black Lace

A Make You Mine Romance

KIMBERLEY ANNE

Cover design by Judith San Nicolas
Typeset in Avenir Next LT Pro 26pt/Centaur 11pt
Printed and bound in Australia by IngramSpark
Prepared for publication and edited by Dr Juliette Lachemeier @ The Erudite Pen: theeruditepen.com

A catalogue record for this book is available from the National Library of Australia

Black Lace: A Make You Mine Romance - Book Three in the Acoustic Series
First ed.
ISBN 9780645784541
E-ISBN 9780645784558

To my family ♥ Thank you for your continued support as I make my dreams a reality.

To my readers ♥ Your support inspires me to continue writing.

A Make You Mine Romance

Book Three

Acoustic Novel Series

Prologue

Lex Black, May 2018

I hit the answer button on my phone. Bringing it to my ear, I greeted the person on the other end and listened to what they had to say.

'Alex Black?' said a man with enough confidence in his voice that made me think that I was in trouble. God, I hoped that wasn't the case. I really hoped I wasn't in trouble. But I guess only time would tell.

There was no point if I only nodded my head, no one could hear it. I would have to verbally answer. 'Yes,' I squeaked out, the clout I usually spoke with was gone. The way he said my name stirred emotions I shouldn't feel while I was at work. I detested the effect this man was having over me while we were on the phone.

I mentally bashed myself as I needed to be more careful when I answered the phone. The use of my full name would always make me shudder from top to toe, even now at twenty-four years of age. Especially when my name came out sounding official.

When my name was said so formally, I was either in trouble or someone wanted something from me. Well, not me, physically. I wasn't the type of woman who put out − ever − it was usually my profession they wanted me for. I much preferred that everyone called me Lex.

'There's some details that need to be exchanged in regards to Ms James,' the man said into my ear, and that was where I felt the need to stop this conversation.

'Harley's trust?'

The man on the other end of the phone went silent. I knew I had interrupted his spiel and that was enough to give me the upper hand to find my sass and regain control of how I was feeling. Of the feelings he was awakening inside me.

'Yes,' I heard grumbled in my ear.

'Well, the next words out of your mouth better explain who you are and what this call is about.' There it was, my sass was back. In my mind, I high-fived myself.

There was a brief silence between us, and I waited patiently.

'Alex, I'm sorry.'

Wow, an apology. Do not interrupt the man. Let him speak. You did after all just ask the man to tell you who he was. 'This is Brad Waters. Ms James is a client. She informed me that your services were to be included on her trust paperwork.'

'Yes, Harley contacted me,' I huffed out to Mr Waters, my sass in full swing now.

'Are we on first-name bases?'

Did Brad not realise how well I knew Harley? I rolled my eyes at the sass given back to me. It was time to be professional.

'Mr Waters, what is the reason for your call?' I dropped my sass and changed my tone. I wanted to let the man know I meant business.

The voice on the other end had gone silky soft. 'Please call me Brad.'

His words were gentle. They made me jittery and gooey at the same time. Something I hadn't felt before. Confident businesswomen who were climbing corporate ladders didn't get the jitters or go gooey, I needed to remind myself.

I don't know you, I started to say, then stopped. 'I...' was the only word that left my mouth before I pulled my lips closed. What was wrong with me? *Get it together.*

'Alex, please, no one calls me Mr Waters. Only my father gets called Mr Waters. Everyone calls me Brad. Please call me Brad.' He took a breath and continued to talk. 'Anyway, I have paperwork that Harley would like me to pass along to you.' There was a small pause in the words that came out of Mr Waters' mouth and that was my cue to jump in.

'Mr Waters,' I said evenly.

'Yes,' he said, and I could sense his curiosity.

'If you want me to call you Brad, then I insist you call me Lex. Never use my full name again, please.' I wanted to say why but I didn't feel that comfortable with this man, a complete stranger.

'We'll see.' Did the man just smirk at me? His words shot straight to my core and made me squirm.

After a moment's silence, I heard. 'Could you come past my office and pick up the paperwork?'

My guess was this man was busy, but did he know that I too was also a busy woman? I took a moment to think about the answer I wanted to give. We did need to meet, this much was true. I needed the paperwork he had, but I also wanted to see what the man was like when I was standing in front of him. Was he as hot in person as he sounded on the phone?

Before I was given the hurry up, I said. 'I'll stop by no later than the close of business today.'

'Thank you, Alex.' The sound of my name made my lips curl up into a smile and gave me jitters more intense than a moment ago. I had to hold my palm flat against my stomach to try and stop what I felt. Did the man not understand I didn't want to be called Alex?

'Okay, Brad, I'll see you later.' The words came out a little breathless. No one had ever gotten to me like that before, especially over the phone.

I hung up without a goodbye. We both knew the conversation was over. I took a deep breath in and cursed myself. Fuck, did I need to get a grip and fast if I was to be able to collect paperwork from his office and make it out in one piece.

I ran my fingers over my scalp and pulled on the hair that was tied up there. I didn't stress that my hair was wrecked, as it helped when you started the day with your hair in a messy bun. Today I chose to work from home at my inner Melbourne city apartment, so I leaned back into the chair I sat in and mentally took stock of the jobs I now had.

Black's Bar and Grill and Little Beats – my brother Zach's businesses. The James Family Trust that included James Family Bakery and two properties that belonged to Harley's mother Mia James. Now Mr Brad Waters was following up on The

Harley James Trust as per Harley's request to have me included as her accountant.

Then there was Connor's money, the money he had profited from the sale of all his businesses. I needed more than the time I had spent combing through his accounts, but I would get to it. But in the meantime, he needed to balance his finances the way a financial planner would, so I set up an investment portfolio for him. Plus, I had a full-time job as a corporate accountant. If I took on anymore side businesses, something in my life would have to give.

I turned my attention back to the job at hand: my full-time job. I had transactions to categorise, expenses to journal and spreadsheets to fill out before I made phone calls and sent emails. So I needed my head to be in the game. Not in fairy-land, daydreaming of what the man I had just spoken to on the phone looked like. It took me the rest of the day to get through the calls, the emails, the spreadsheets, journals and transactions.

By the time four p.m. rolled around, I was in need of a little something to take the edge off. Something a little stronger than the coffee I had drunk today. I had a lot on my plate, and I realised it was only getting bigger. A change in career was a lot to think about. But eventually I would need to do something about my ever-growing side hustle.

I left my car parked in the underground carpark of the apartment complex that I lived in. There were eight apartments; six I knew had tenants and two I had never seen anyone go in or come out of. There were four private rentals, two on the ground level and two on the first level.

My brother Zach and I had been gifted our apartments on the top and second levels respectively, from our parents, as they owned the whole complex. I wasn't privy to why there were

5

empty apartments in our complex, but I guess my parents had their reasons.

I rugged myself up and let myself out of my apartment with my leather laptop work tote in tow for the paperwork I was about to stow in there. You never knew what the weather would be like in inner-city Melbourne. I took the stairs down to the street, checked my phone for the address Brad Waters had given me and headed out on foot in his direction.

I was a million miles away, lost in thought when I felt a shoulder bump mine. I wanted to turn around grab the fingers on the person that had touched me and bend them back until I heard the slightest crack. But I didn't do that.

I did, however, stop and turn around. I opened my mouth then closed it as quickly as I could. The man that had just collided with me was the tallest, sexiest, well-built man in a suit I had ever seen. And he had his hand on my forearm. I wanted to shake him off, but I didn't. I let him touch me a little longer. Something I should've known better from the black belt in Brazilian Jiu-Jitsu I had.

The man in front of me gave me the once-over to check to see if I were okay, and all I could do was blush from the way he looked at me. I stepped back so I didn't have to crank my neck to look up into the most beautiful green eyes.

'I'm sorry.' The man in front of me said as he let go of my arm.

I missed his touch already, and that was through the layers of clothes I had on. I didn't even know this man yet his touch had me weak at the knees.

What was wrong with me? First the phone call this morning and now this man. Maybe it had been too long, and my body had something to say on the matter of sexy voices and well-dressed men. Pity they couldn't have been from the same man.

'I'm okay.' I found my voice to tell the mystery man in front of me.

'No damage done then,' the very cute stranger said with his best smile, and I almost melted inside – another gooey moment. 'If you're okay, I do have to run. I'm late for my next appointment. See you around.'

'I'm fine.' I returned the smile and then the mystery man was gone.

The smile on my face lasted the rest of the way to the office block Brad said he worked out of. His office wasn't far and when I saw that someone had witnessed my exchange with the cute, mysterious stranger, my smile faded at the look on their face. Distaste oozed from his features. I could see he wasn't very happy. *Was the distaste with me? Probably.*

'I take it you enjoyed the show?' I said, but really shouldn't have. I was supposed to be in professional mode. My business hat was supposed to be on.

'Best to stay away from those who would only use you before they squashed you like a bug.' The sexy timbre was the same as this morning when we had spoken on the phone.

'Who that guy? You know him?'

He nodded. 'He has a reputation, and not a good one.'

'I appreciate your concern, but I think I can take care of myself. Thank you, though, for the heads up.' I tried the business approach and avoided the sass, but I didn't quite get there.

'Don't say I didn't warn you, Alex.' I knew we hadn't been formally introduced but I didn't have to wonder how he knew who I was. He had met Zach after all, and my brothers and I did share similar features. Brown hair, brown eyes.

There was a silence between us now that we were face to face. Something I didn't think would happen after our phone conversation this morning. I stood a few steps away and gave the man that stood in front of me the once over.

He was taller than my hundred and seventy centimetres, and it made me wonder how many inches he was past six foot. His features were similar to Henry Cavill's. Brad Waters wore a black suit, just like the stranger who had bumped into me. But Brad's wasn't a designer suit, and his tie had been pulled down, a sign it was the end of his day.

There was something about Brad that made him a little rugged even though he was clean shaven. His face didn't show distaste now, just a raised eyebrow and a hint of a smirk that let me know he was curious. *Could he be curious about me?* I curved my lips upwards to show off my most genuine smile.

'If you lick your lips, I'd be tempted to think that you might eat me.'

I was tempted to stick my tongue out one more time just to see what he would do. A little curious to see his reaction.

But instead of licking my lips, I said, 'You must be Mr Waters.'

'I am, which makes you Ms Black.' Brad held out a hand for me to shake and when I did, I felt a spark at our touch that made me want to jump back and away from our held hands. Brad let go of my hand first, and it made me wonder if he felt the same zap.

'It's been a long day, so please let me take you for a drink and we can talk about the paperwork I'm about to give you.'

'Okay,' I agreed, and I didn't even know why.

Maybe it was because I too had had a long day. Maybe I just needed that drink to take off the edge. Maybe I wanted to know more about this man. So, I followed Brad to a little bar not far from his office, where we had a few too many drinks and talked well into the evening, not just about the line of business we were in.

Sparks flew between and around us, and I let Brad take my hand and lead me to his apartment, where I pressed my lips to his. It was a kiss that turned hungry and left us breathless and our clothes on the floor. Picking me up and laying me down, I was cherished from top to toe. I was sated in such a way that I knew one night with this man would never be enough.

One

Lex Black, June 2018

'What the fuck, Connor?' Were the words that came out of my mouth as soon as I opened the front door to the holiday house I owned. The two-storey house that once belonged to my parents was my home away from home. It sat on the edge of the Murray River in the little country town I grew up in – Mulwala. My hometown was a place that held so many family memories I treasured dearly, which I always wanted to hold on to.

This house would always be a sanctuary for my family and me when we needed an escape from the real world. It had been a while since I had been here, needing a break from my life in the city. It was why I told Connor he could stay here while he got his shit together. I really hoped I didn't regret it. *Could*

Connor handle me as housemate if I decided I wanted to stay a little while?

I stormed through the house and stood by the island bench in the kitchen and waited for my brother. I knew my words had woken him as they had come out a little tight, a little strained. It wasn't very often my help was requested without receiving any further detail. Connor owed me an explanation. I needed to find out from Connor what the hell had happened and what he needed my help for.

'Alex!' My name clipped out at me just above a whisper.

I turned to face my brother. My sunglass-covered eyes gave him the once over.

'Everyone is asleep, or I hope they still are. Can you keep it down?'

'What the hell happened?' I asked Connor, but by the look of him, he was too tired to talk, and I wouldn't get anything out of him if I pushed him too hard when he looked like I felt. Shit.

'I know you want to know. But I can't do this right now.' My brother's words confirmed my thoughts.

'Fine,' I told Connor. 'I'll be at Zach's.'

'Thanks, Lex.' Connor reached out and wrapped me up in his arms.

I felt a single tear well in my eye then roll down my cheek at the smallest amount of affection my brother offered. He didn't know, and I couldn't really blame him for his lack of attention to detail towards me. I would be stupid if I didn't recognise that he had his own drama to deal with. He didn't need to worry about mine as well.

I let go of my brother and headed for the front door. I closed the door as quietly as possible and made my way over to my suped-up black Commodore wagon and got in the passenger seat. I didn't even have to say a word before my car was in gear and was on a roll out of my driveway. I didn't even have to say where I wanted to go. Or give the directions on how to get there either. I just knew that was where my car was headed.

'You want to talk about it?' I was asked. His words filled the silence in my own car.

'No,' I tried to say as calmly as I could, but it didn't come out that way. Now I felt like a bitch for the cold shoulder I gave off. But I couldn't help the mood I was in at the moment.

'I won't push you to talk to me about whatever is going on in that pretty head of yours, or whatever this is between us, Alex.'

I didn't know how I felt about the use of the name my parents had given me in a setting this intimate, as everyone called me Lex. I was only ever called Alex when I was in trouble.

'I know you have a lot on your plate right now. Just please don't shut me out. I can be the shoulder you lean on.'

I felt a hand reach for mine, the sensation stopping my thoughts dead in their tracks. When fingers entwined with mine and my fingers were kissed, I went with the flow of the moment, and just let my hand be held and the feeling of his lips on my skin wash over me. It had been a while since I had been this intimate with anyone.

More silence filled the inside of my car, and I didn't respond. I didn't know how to. I was saved by my car as it pulled up to the front of Zach and Harley's house. I was relieved as we parked alongside my brother's suped-up black Chevrolet and his girlfriend's grey Impreza hatchback.

The front door of the house opened before I could even get out of my car and knock on the door. Zach had made himself comfortable as he leant up against the frame of his front door.

His reaction when I got out of the passenger seat made me wonder. Would he approve that someone else was here with me, that someone else sat behind the wheel of my beloved car?

I made a move to get out when I noticed the doors were locked and the door handle wouldn't let me out. My hand was still held by the person in the driver's seat. I turned my full attention to my right and opened my mouth to speak, but no sound came out.

A hand cupped my neck and pulled me closer towards lips I had kissed before, but did I really want them to kiss me now? I guess I was about to find out. Our foreheads and noses touched. Our lips didn't. I felt the tears well, but I didn't want them to fall right now.

I tried to hold them back, but when his lips touched my forehead, it was just the right amount of affection to make me lose it. Tears fell in a steady stream from my eyes and now I was a blubbery mess – right before I was about to get out of my car to see my brother and his girlfriend Harley.

'I'm not going to promise everything will be okay. I will just *make* everything okay.' At the edge of my sunglasses, thumbs wiped away my tears as words filled my car.

There was a sad smile on my face when we moved away from each other. With no words to say, I turned my head towards the passenger door and when I tried the handle this time, the door opened.

Zach's reaction to my situation will be interesting, I thought to myself, to take my mind off the mess I was in. I pushed the door open wide and stepped out.

'Harley!' Zach turned his head and yelled into the house, and a moment later she was tucked up under his arm where she would always belong.

At the sight of me as I closed the passenger door, Harley was on the move down the steps and was headed in my direction. She didn't offer any verbal hellos, but wrapped me up in her arms and squeezed me tight.

Harley offered the one thing I had needed the most – a security bubble – the same as my brother offered her. Maybe she sensed I was a little off, then again maybe she didn't. Harley let go of our embrace, took a hold of my hand and walked me up the steps towards the front door.

'Who drove your car, Lex?' my brother asked me as I approached.

But I didn't get to answer. The driver chose the moment I reached my brother to open the driver's side door to get out.

'Brad Waters?' my brother questioned me. 'He drove you up from Melbourne?'

'Zach!' Harley said my brother's name to warn him to tread lightly.

'Please don't be too hard on him.' I stared up at my brother and kissed his cheek before I continued. 'He is not the reason for the mess I'm in.'

Whether or not the words I just told Zach registered inside his head, I would never know. But when he didn't jump off the front veranda to try and kill Brad, I breathed out the relief I didn't know I needed. I didn't get to see the interaction between Zach and Brad, as Harley had pulled me inside the house and over to the lounge in the family room.

I didn't even make it to the lounge before the tears started to fall again.

'Lex,' Harley said my name softly. Her tone soothed a part inside me, and I wondered if this was what it was like to have a sister.

We sat down on the lounge. Harley still had a hold of my hand. Neither of us spoke, and I was okay with that for now. But I knew at some stage I would have to let it all out. If not some of it.

Two

Lex Black

Harley must have read my mind. She took off towards the kitchen and a moment later she was back with coffee in her hands. I took the cup she offered with both hands then took a sip.

Harley had made me one of her specials — a latte with a touch of hazelnut syrup and a dusting of chocolate powder on top. Harley had been experimenting with her coffee-making, adding in different flavours. I smiled on the inside, but it must have shown on my face too, and when I looked at Harley, she smiled back. I couldn't help but wonder if we reminisced about the same thing.

'Spill, girlfriend,' were Harley's words to me. 'Take off those damn sunglasses and talk to me.'

I didn't take off my sunglasses, I just shook my head, not sure why I couldn't find my voice.

'It's okay,' Harley's voice was soft. 'Please tell me what just made you smile?'

'That you're happy,' I croaked out through my sniffles. I took a deep breath before I added, 'All of it. My brother, our hometown, this cup of coffee. It looks good on you.'

'You would look as good as me if you lived here,' Harley joked, and I knew she just wanted to make me laugh. But all I could manage was the same small smile.

'Maybe,' I whispered. Harley's words made me think that she was right. Maybe I did need a change of scene.

The smile that lit up Harley's face almost reached her ears, and her eyes shone. She really was jubilant here. My brother added to her bliss. I wanted to feel like that, not this scared version of myself.

'We love each other. That much is true. And we are incredibly happy. But it hasn't always been that way, as you know.' Harley glowed as she spoke about her relationship with my brother. 'One day you will find a love like that. Maybe you brought him with you, Lex.' Harley definitely had her rose-coloured glasses on, but perhaps there was some truth to Harley's words. Brad and I had been spending more time together getting to know each other.

I wasn't in a place where I believed in true love the way Harley did. I didn't even know how I felt about Brad. All I knew was, in this moment, things in my life were one giant mess and I needed to sort them out.

'Hey,' Harley said to me as she took my cup and placed it on the coffee table in front of us. 'You will find your true love. I know it, and I believe it.'

I took a moment to let Harley's words sink in, and when they did, I felt more tears flow down my face. Harley moved close enough to wrap her arm around me and when she was comfortable in my personal space, I felt her fingers slide my sunglasses off my face.

The gasp Harley let out didn't startle me. I knew how bad it looked, but her exclamation raised the attention of my brother and Brad. The men moved closer but didn't say a word. No doubt their eyes were glued to my face before I covered it with both of my hands.

I knew Brad took a seat next to me, and his hand automatically rubbed my shoulder. I could only assume Zach had sat down next to Harley. But I didn't really know, face in my hands or not. It didn't matter as I couldn't see through my swollen eye and bruised face.

'Zach.' Harley kissed his cheek then whispered, 'Get some ice and a towel for Lex, please.'

Zach didn't say anything, though I knew he wanted to. He just got up and did what she'd asked. Harley knew how protective Zach was of me, so maybe she knew he would need a minute to cool off too.

As Harley removed the arm she had around me, I felt one touch replaced with another, and two stronger arms wrapped me up and pulled me onto his lap. I couldn't help but lean in a little and lay my head on Brad's shoulder. In my fragile state, I liked the way it felt. It was nice to lean on someone and in return have someone comfort me.

'I'm here. You're safe. I won't let him hurt you again,' Brad whispered into the shell of my ear. At the promise I heard, I couldn't help but move my hands, one under Brad's arm where it cupped his shoulder, and the other to the hem of his tee-shirt where I held on for dear life.

From the moment my hands moved away from my face, I felt the coldness on my skin. Ice soothed the soreness of my swollen eye and bruised cheek. When the coldness wore off and my face had gone numb, I pushed the wrapped-up ice away.

But I dared not to move from the spot I was in. Brad's arms were still wrapped around me, and I never wanted to leave the protective bubble that he had put me in. This moment with Brad felt too good. Almost like I belonged here.

The silence lasted while the ice numbed my face. Then I heard, 'Lex, what the fuck? What happened!' I knew my brother couldn't help himself. I knew it would eat away at him until he got his chance to ask.

'I let myself fall for the charms of a man whose true colours were unnerving,' I told my brother amidst the turmoil of my emotions. I paced my breaths, and a few tears escaped before I continued. 'Not even with my training did I sense he would hurt me until it was almost too late.'

'Lex, what does that even mean?' I could hear the slight frustration in Zach's voice and when I didn't answer, Zach tried his luck and turned his attention to Brad in the hope that he would get something. 'Brad?' But Brad didn't answer Zach either.

Amidst the silence and the tension I had created, I closed my eyes to block everything out. I didn't know how exactly Brad knew I had had enough, but he did. I felt Brad lift me off the lounge and carry me towards one of the two spare bedrooms Zach and Harley had in their house.

I didn't know which room Brad had chosen to lay me down in. All I knew was that we were alone. Brad pulled back the doona and gently placed me on the sheet-covered mattress. He rolled the blinds down and drew the curtains closed. I didn't know what his plans were now, but I didn't want to be alone.

'Please don't leave,' I whispered into the quiet room. 'I don't want to be alone.'

'Baby cakes, you couldn't get rid of me if you tried.' The words didn't shock me, not really, especially when he called me baby cakes. I kind of liked the endearment he had chosen for me, but I really liked that he wanted to hang around too.

I kicked out of my shoes as Brad sat on the edge of the bed to do the same. I found the middle of the bed and curled into a ball on my right side, my bruised cheek and swollen eye exposed.

Brad waited patiently for me to get comfortable before he climbed in beside me and pulled the doona cover over us. We lay face to face in silence for what seemed like a long time but was really only a couple of minutes.

'You told me he would squash me like a bug,' I croaked out, my throat sore from all my tears. If I could be any harder on myself for what I had gotten myself in to, I probably would have worn out the carpet in Zach and Harley's house. All I needed was the energy to do it.

'Shh,' Brad soothed as he brushed a hand over the back of my head. 'He only squashed you a little and he can't hurt you anymore,' Brad whispered to me as his forehead touched mine.

'What if you hadn't turned up when you did and scared him off? What would have happened?' I asked, completely unsure of myself. Somewhere between the lounge and the bedroom my tears had dried up.

'I will always be here for you, baby cakes.' Brad brushed his thumb along the edge of my face and avoided my bruised cheek.

I wanted to believe it was true; maybe I would when I wasn't being too hard on myself.

'He may have had you pinned, but I saw the way you had hold of his hand as I came up the stairs. I heard the crack of his bones as you pushed him away. You're going to be sore for a couple of days, but so is he. You got him good.'

I tried to smile at Brad's words. 'My face is sore,' I admitted.

'I can get you more ice,' Brad said as he made a move to get off the bed.

'Later.' I reached my fingers out to Brad's forearm. I didn't want him to get off this bed. Not yet anyway.

'Okay.' He settled back in bed next to me.

'I'm sorry I didn't tell you how bad it was,' I said of my eye and cheek.

'Did he you hurt anywhere else?'

'I wasn't even paying attention. My head was down. I just wanted to get home after I called you. He surprised me when he turned me around and that's when he landed the first blow, a backhand to my cheek. We sparred for a few minutes before he overpowered me and pinned me down, and that's when he punched me in the eye. He was about to land another blow to my face when I grabbed his hand and bent his fingers back until I heard the crack.'

'Show me. I want to see where he hit you.'

Moving to turn on the lamp, Brad watched as I removed my clothes until all that was left was my underwear. Small bruises had started to form from where I had sparred with a man who'd tried to squash me.

'I want to kill that motherfucker for every one of these marks on your body,' Brad said as his protectiveness once again kicked in. He came closer to kiss my forehead, and at the feel of warmth on my skin, my hand reached out and touched his chest. Picking up my hand to entwine our fingers, Brad proceeded to place his lips on the discolouration that was forming on my torso.

'Don't give up on me,' were the last words I said into the darkness before I drifted off into sleep.

'Never,' I heard whispered as Brad rested my hand back on his chest.

Three

Brad Waters

I lay in bed face to face with Alex Black. I didn't know why she'd picked me to call last night. But I was glad she did. Ever since I'd handed over the paperwork to Harley's trust, I hadn't been able to get her off my mind.

Alex was the one woman that had given me a run for my money in hard work and intelligence. We'd met on Fridays for a few drinks at the end of each week to catch up, and every week Alex would let me take her back to my apartment, to recreate our first time together. It always started with the same hungry meeting of our lips. Alex had only stayed the first night; she had fallen into organismic bliss, and I got to lay with my arm around her all night. Since then, Alex had come up with an excuse to leave before she fell asleep.

And now I got to lay here with Alex while her hand rested on my chest as she drifted off to sleep. My hand covered hers, and I brought her fingers to my lips to kiss before I put her hand back on my chest. I wanted to stay here like this forever, right next to her, but I knew she needed more ice on her bruised face.

I waited for Alex's breath to even out before I softly pressed my lips to her forehead and made a move off the bed. When Alex didn't protest, I made my way to the kitchen for more ice when I was bailed up by an angry Zach.

'Brad,' he clipped.

Alex's brother didn't scare or intimidate me, and before I spoke, I cupped Zach's shoulder. 'I know I just showed up out of the blue with your sister bruised and battered, and I get that you want to know what happened. But Alex needs to recover, and right now she's asleep and she needs more ice for her face. You can get her side of what happened when she wakes up.' They were the words I had for Zach as I refilled the zip-lock bag with ice and wrapped the now wet towel around it.

Zach nodded his head. He didn't push for more as he watched me walk away from him and towards the bedroom where Alex was asleep. I resumed my position next to her on the bed as I placed the ice over her eye and cheek. Alex squirmed at the coldness on her face but didn't open her eyes. I lay with her until her face should have been numb, then I pulled the towel-covered ice away.

This time when I left the comfort of the room Alex was asleep in, I knew wouldn't have a choice but to tell Harley and Zach about what had happened to the woman asleep. I kissed Alex's forehead once more before I got off the bed and tucked the doona around her.

I ran my fingers up over my unshaven face and through my hair that was longer on top and shorter on the sides, then I took a deep breath as I moved away from the bed. I softly closed the bedroom door and found Harley and Zach next to each other on the lounge in their family room. Talking.

'Don't feel bad, Zach. Alex is a grown woman, and she can take care of herself. She wouldn't want you hovering around her anyway.'

'I do feel bad, Harley.' Frustration was evident in Zach's voice. 'I chose to stay in Mulwala when Connor and Lex wanted to move to Melbourne. But staying here meant not being able to protect Lex.'

'Zach,' Harley tried to soothe the man she loved but it fell on deaf ears.

As soon as Zach had seen me, he didn't beat around the bush. He pounced, turning his irritation my way. 'How badly is she hurt? Is she okay? She called you when she was in trouble. Are you two friends or is there something more going on?'

Zach's questions didn't surprise me. He had every right to be worried about his younger sister, especially after the night she'd just experienced and was now looking worse for wear.

'I like your sister,' I told him honestly. 'I will always be there for her, but if she wants something more, the ball is in her court. I won't ever rush her. Your sister has a few bruises on her torso from where they sparred, and she will be sore for a couple of days.'

'What happened?' Harley asked, a shocked tone in her voice. 'How did Lex end up with a battered face?'

'I didn't know about her face until you took off her sunglasses. I'm as shocked as you,' I admitted, answering Harley's question.

I breathed in a deep breath and then breathed out before I said. 'Alex called me from Little Beats. She was there for a couple of end-of-week drinks with a client she wanted to woo for work. Said she was on her way home but that something didn't feel right. Something in Alex's voice sounded off. She sounded shaken,' I told Zach and Harley.

'Then what happened?' Zach huffed out some of his frustration.

'I hightailed my arse over to Alex's apartment. When I got there, they were sparring, but he had the upper hand and was about to land a blow to her face when she grabbed his hand and twisted it until she heard it crack. That's when I yelled out, and Alex pushed him off her then scampered backwards, and he took off. ' I paused my recollection of last night to tap into my anger. 'I didn't know Alex had already been hit in the face. By the time we got inside her apartment, her phone had all of her attention.'

'Yeah, that was me,' Zach admitted to me. 'I wanted to fill Lex in on what had happened at The Grand Hotel. I knew Lex would want to help.'

'Well, her phone definitely gave her something to fixate on. She packed her bags and begged me to drive her here. But I told her she needed to calm down, so we argued, and she stomped off to her room. I slept on her lounge. There was no way was I about to leave her alone. She woke me up a little over four hours ago and here we are.'

No way did I tell them that Alex's screams woke me up. I had lain down next to her and wrapped my arm around her. I whispered sweet nothings in her ear until she calmed down and went back to sleep.

'Did you say Lex had twisted the guy's hand until it cracked?' Harley asked, and she seemed surprised. Zach didn't though.

'Yeah,' I said as I remembered what I'd found as I came up the steps from the ground level to the first floor of Alex's apartment complex. 'She had that look in her eyes, like she wanted to break every bone in his body, but he was too strong for her.'

'Wow!' Harley stated. 'Remind me not to get on Lex's bad side.'

'Harley,' Zach said in his girlfriend's direction. 'Lex is disciplined. She won't ever hurt you.' Zach's words told me he knew the same thing or two about self-defence that Alex did.

Was I surprised that Alex knew how to take care of herself? When I considered we didn't really know each other, the answer had to be no.

'I know Lex would never hurt me,' I heard Harley tell Zach. But I tuned them out when I felt my phone vibrate in my pocket. I couldn't ignore the calls any longer.

I pulled my phone from my pocket and got lost in what I saw. The home screen was full of missed calls and text messages. I unlocked the phone to check the missed calls, and they had all come from the one number. I scrolled through the string of text messages that had been left. The firm I worked for had a new case and I was needed, apparently. Although I didn't understand why my team couldn't work through this one without me. That was why I had a team to work through things when I couldn't. Otherwise, what was the point?

I needed to respond but didn't want to. I was torn between Alex and my job. A job I would give up in a heartbeat for the woman that was asleep right now. If I could, I would do it all tonight. Quit for Alex. That told me I was in deeper than I thought. Alex had really gotten to me. I had fallen hard. And all we had shared were a few dreamy nights. I should have known our end of the week hook-ups would never be enough.

B: I'm out of town. Let my team handle it.

I sent my response, and my phone vibrated almost immediately in my hand. My response obviously wasn't good enough. I stood up and excused myself. 'Sorry, I have to take this.' I made my way to the glass door in the kitchen that would let me out on to the back veranda.

'I wouldn't go out there,' Harley said when my hand landed on the door handle. 'Okay.' I dropped my hand and walked over to the front door. Opening it, I slipped out, then answered the phone and took a seat on the front steps of the veranda.

I didn't even get to speak. As soon as my phone reached my ear, I heard the person on the other end start to talk. 'Where are you?'

'Out of town,' I clipped out my reply.

'We have a new case.' The caller was firm.

'Then my team can handle it.' I threw out the words and hoped they stuck.

'I need you on this, and it would be best if you were there from the start.' I gathered my team couldn't handle it. This case had better be worth it, that's if I was able to leave Alex here with her brother and his girlfriend.

'Details?' I asked, though I don't know why I caved.

'There's a meeting tomorrow, first thing.' When wasn't there a meeting about something, first thing?

I gave in because maybe this was my chance to wrap up my cases. 'I'll be there.'

My huff of annoyance went unnoticed by the person on the other end of the phone. Frustration wasted.

The line had gone dead. My last words were obviously the right ones to say.

I put my phone in my pocket and made my way back inside. I moved straight to the bedroom where Alex was asleep. Kneeling on the carpeted floor, I held Alex's hand. Then I leant in and softly pressed my lips to her lips to kiss her my goodbye.

'Sorry, baby cakes. I've been summoned back to Melbourne. I don't want to leave you, but you are in good hands with your brother and Harley.' I knew Alex hadn't heard the words I had just told her. I didn't want to leave her, but I had a job to do.

'Something has come up and I'm needed back in Melbourne. I need to take Alex's car. I'll try to come back in a couple of days. While I'm gone can you make sure Alex doesn't do anything stupid,' I said to Harley and Zach when I reached the family room. They had resumed their earlier discussion.

'You know, she wanted me to bring her up here last night, but I told her she needed to rest and that I would drive her up first thing this morning. Last night has shaken her up badly, but she is right where she needs to be with you and Harley.'

'I appreciate you for being there for Lex when I couldn't be. Thank you for bringing her here. I'll make sure she's okay and doesn't do anything foolish.'

'Sure,' I said, heading towards the front door.

'You know Lex will want answers when she wakes up,' Zach said as he followed me out to Alex's car.

'I know Alex will want a shoulder to lean when she wakes up, and I'm sorry I won't be here for the aftermath. But she will be okay as long as she isn't left alone.'

'Knowing Lex, she will throw herself into what she does best: her work. I'll keep my eye on her.'

I pulled out the bags Alex had put in the boot of her car and handed them over for Zach to take. We shook hands before I left Zach on his front steps to head back to Melbourne.

Four

Lex

My body thrashed left then right, but I didn't scream before I bolted upright. A sheen of sweat covered my chest. My attack played on repeat behind closed eyelids, my attacker's face clear as day burnt into my memory.

My worst nightmare, and no one was here to comfort me. The room I slept in was dark, and I could sense that I was alone. Where the hell was Brad when I needed him to chase this nightmare away? When I wanted his arms around me?

I sat tangled in the doona of this spare bed with a wet towel in my lap. I wasn't sure when more ice was put on my face. I moved off the bed in search of something. Something to comfort me.

'Hello.' You could hear that I had been asleep as my voice was a little groggy.

I walked from one end of my brother's house to the other. It was very quiet in here. No one answered my hello. I was alone and I didn't really want to be.

Zach, Harley and Brad were all gone, and I wasn't sure why. Zach's minibar caught my eye. I knew it was the last thing I should do, but I couldn't help myself; plus, there was no one here to stop me.

I searched all the bottles that Zach kept in his minibar on the edge of his kitchen. I found an opened bottle of black labelled Jim Beam and took it. *I could handle half a bottle,* I told myself.

A drink or two would knock off the edge of how I felt right now about being alone. More than a few drinks would make me numb and that was where I wanted to be if I was going to be here by myself. I didn't want to feel the way I'd felt when my attacker touched me. The first time he'd laid his palm on my forearm, I'd felt tingles, but now I just felt skin burning. I didn't want to think about Brad Waters either, or the way his touch seemed to linger in a sheen of tingles and soothed the burning parts of me.

I tucked the bottle under my arm and made my way outside into the sunshine. Stepping through the glass doors of the kitchen, I looked up towards the sky and let the sunshine hit my face and warm my body.

I scoured the backyard and made my way towards a shady patch on the grass. I felt Abby's eyes follow me down towards the place I wanted to sit, but Zach's dog didn't move from her sunny spot on the back veranda.

In the most ungracious way, I plopped myself down on the grass and took the lid off the bottle. Taking a swig, I let the alcohol burn its way down my throat. I held back the cough my body wanted to let go of and breathed in then out, and before I chickened out, I took another swig.

The second swallow didn't burn as much, so I took swig after swig until I didn't feel anything at all. I only realised I had taken my pity party too far when my head hit the grass, and everything had gone as dark as my surname. Black.

'Alex,' I heard yelled, though it sounded so far away. 'Alex,' I heard again, and this time hands shook my body. *No, I don't think so. No one got to touch me.* Now that I had been attacked, being manhandled didn't feel right.

I came to. Confused. Maybe it was because I didn't feel so great. I made my move, and eyes closed, I pushed my hands up until I reached the person who was touching me. I pushed again, catching the other person off guard. My legs wrapped around a torso, and I forced myself to roll over to gain the upper hand.

But I didn't have the upper hand, I was too sluggish. *Damn you, alcohol.* My response was too slow. We had rolled over again, and now I was on my back. Hands reached out to pin both of my shoulders, but I didn't want to be pinned down.

My legs unwrapped from around the torso. I brought my knees to my chest and planted my feet on the chest of the body that was on top of me. I pushed with all that I had into a backwards somersault and landed on top this time.

'What the hell, Zach?' someone screamed towards me. 'Jesus Christ, Alex!'

Those words stopped me in my tracks, and I'm grateful they did, because with all of the motions I had just made, I now felt dizzy and woozy. *Oh my God, I think I might throw up.* I didn't open my eyes. I just rolled off who I had a hold of and onto my side.

My head touched the grass, but it didn't stop the dizziness. It didn't even slow it down. I couldn't stop what happened next and didn't know how many times I vomited. But I did. All the alcohol I had just drunk was now in a pile on the lawn in Zach's backyard.

'Harley, where have you been?' Was the question I heard asked from beside me.

'I'm sorry, I fell asleep. I didn't know I wouldn't hear Alex when she woke up,' Harley admitted, her voice was softer now it was closer.

'Lexie,' was quietly whispered into my ear when I was picked up from the ground to be carried inside. I knew that nickname. Zach used his childhood nickname for me. He was the only one I ever let call me that name.

'I don't want to be alone,' I said over and over. 'Please don't leave me alone.' I cried into Zach's shoulder, and he held me a little tighter.

I hadn't opened my eyes, and I didn't know why I couldn't. Was I embarrassed? Ashamed? Afraid? Maybe I was a little of everything. I knew I needed to cool my jets, and the bathroom floor was always good for that.

I felt myself being lowered down into what I didn't know until I felt the spray hit my face. I struggled to take in air around the water from the shower until I opened my eyes and realised I had to move.

Zach stood and watched me through the closed glass shower door. He left to where I wasn't sure, then he was back with a bucket in his hand.

He left the bucket on the floor close to the shower, then he walked out. Was he mad? Did I hurt him? Did I hurt myself? There was a fog in my head that wouldn't let me answer those questions. *Damn you, alcohol,* I cursed again. But it wasn't the alcohol I should have been cursing. It was myself I needed to berate.

I let the water saturate my clothes, my face and hair before I reached up and turned it off. I pushed open the shower door and crawled out of the shower then lay there on the floor for who knows how long. I dry-heaved over the bucket a few times, grateful there was nothing left in my stomach. Stripping out of my wet clothes, I took a hot shower this time to rid my skin and hair of the smell of alcohol and vomit. I dried myself and wrapped the towel around me.

I brushed my teeth to remove the taste that something had died in my mouth. Rinsed and spat. I felt only slightly better, but nowhere near as human as I should be. The alcohol was a mask to cover for the way I felt, hurt from my attack and confused about Brad and what I felt for him.

I left the bathroom for the room Brad had lain me down in earlier today and dressed myself in the clothes that were left for me on the edge of the bed: three-quarter leggings and a long tee-shirt.

When I walked into the kitchen, I saw both Harley and Zach were seated at the kitchen bench. Zach turned in my direction, his arms open wide, and I couldn't help myself but to fall into them.

'I'm sorry, I guess I'm a little lost at the moment,' I admitted.

'Lexie.' Zach gave me squeeze. 'I should know better than to startle you. But you scared me, passed out on the lawn like that.'

'I didn't mean to drink so much. I just wanted to be numb,' I whispered. 'I woke up alone and didn't want to be.'

'I'm sorry, Lex,' Harley told me. 'I'm not sure what's wrong with me. I fell asleep when Zach left to run errands.'

Was there something that Harley was trying to say? I couldn't think clearly in my alcohol haze.

'I knew you were hurting, I just didn't realise how badly.'

I breathed in and took a step away from Zach's embrace for a glass of water. With the water in my hand, I moved over to the lounge and sat down.

Harley and Zach followed me. Then I asked. 'Where's Brad?' *Why was he not here?*

'He took your car to go back to Melbourne,' Harley told me.

'He didn't even say goodbye,' I said, with more emotion than was needed.

'Lex, he said goodbye,' Zach told me. His raised eyebrow questioned me.

'Oh my God!' I exclaimed. 'I thought that was just a dream.' My words left the lips I now touched. I hadn't heard the words he'd said to me, but I'd definitely felt the press of his lips onto mine. Lips that tingled now that I thought about Brad.

'Woman, when are you going to admit you have it bad for that man,' Harley said to me, with her eyebrow raised just like Zach's. 'You do know that man has it just as bad for you.'

There were no words to say to that statement, because then I would have had to admit to myself that I was falling for the man in question. And I didn't know if I was I ready for that. But who was I kidding after all the Friday nights we had been spending together.

Five

Lex

'You want to explain showing up out of the blue and what this afternoon was all about?' Zach asked, and I wondered how long it would be before I was grilled over my actions.

'Something happened for you to want to come to Mulwala,' Harley spoke softly. 'You have a black eye and bruised cheek, you made Brad drive you here, you drank yourself unconscious, and you wrestled your brother. That's not like you.'

Well fuck. How did I do this? Where did I start? I tucked my feet up under me and saw two sets of eyes wait for me to answer. Taking a sip of water then a deep breath, I tried not to let the last twenty-four hours get under my skin and make me emotional and start crying again. But as soon as I opened my mouth, my eyes welled.

'About a month ago on my way to pick up Harley's trust paperwork, I bumped into a man. He made me feel gooey inside, and I thought he might have been the type of man that I wanted. A tall, sexy professional who matched my intellect.'

My long, deep breaths in and slow exhales didn't stop the tears from falling down my face. I had started my explanation now, so I had no choice but to continue.

'He bailed me up two weeks later as I was finishing up with a potential new client at The Coffee House not far from where I work in Collins Street. He insisted I stay and join him for a coffee, but the moment I sat down he fired question after question at me wanting information like I was the only one who could give it to him. I tried my best to deflect. By the time I left I was feeling extremely uncomfortable, and I hadn't been able to shake that feeling. Then last night happened.'

I turned my face away from Zach and Harley and closed my eyes, so I didn't see them move from their spot on the lounge to come and sit beside me. Both wrapped their arms around me and enveloped me in their love and their own protective bubbles. And I must admit I felt slightly better.

'What did he want to know?' Zach asked, a touch of curiosity in his tone.

'He wanted information on Connor. Do you think he's in danger?'

'Connor can take care of himself, and he's not in Melbourne, he's here in Mulwala.'

I felt Zach move away and hold me at arm's length. 'How about the next time you decide on the need to feel numb, why don't you grab your guitar and play something instead?'

Harley let go of me in that moment and got up from the lounge and went in search of something.

Zach gave a light squeeze to my shoulders before he let me go, and my eyes opened to Harley's outstretched arm. She held a guitar in her hand. I let out a ragged breath and took what was offered, though the guitar wasn't mine.

I didn't know where my guitar was. Did I leave it in Melbourne and in my haste to get out of town, forget it? Guess I didn't know how long I would be here now I didn't have my car. At least this borrowed guitar would help me feel a little less lost.

I rested the back of the guitar across my knees and strummed through a couple of cords. It felt good to let go of some of my emotions and gently strum the strings. This guitar would be the lifeline I could count on, because half a bottle of Jim Beam Black sure as hell wasn't any kind of lifeline.

This guitar would be where I turned when I needed comfort that was until I could get to my beloved guitar. Maybe a little downtime would help me sort myself out, the way I felt and what I was going to do with my life from now on.

'Did Brad leave my things?' I asked both Harley and Zach.

'I put them in your room,' Zach told me as I got up from the lounge to go and get my phone.

I stumbled around for my things in the room I'd just slept in. In my franticness and the need to get out of my apartment and away from the last twenty-four hours, I'd packed a bag full of clothes, my handbag with my personal items and a tote with a few things I thought I might need, like my phone, tablet and laptop.

I found my phone on the bottom of my handbag. When I pulled it out and looked at the screen, I could see message after message and a few missed calls. Shit.

Peyton Andrews ran her own firm, Andrews and Co Accounting, and as her employee, I was one of her account managers. Scrolling through my phone, I found the number I wanted and hit call. I rang my boss. She knew I often worked from home a few days a week, but I was expected to call in and give updates or email through a progress report of what I was working on. Today I had done neither.

'Peyton, I know I haven't touched base today.' I stopped for a breath then said with as much energy as I could muster. 'I'll be working from home for the rest of the week.'

'Thanks for reaching out, Lex, to give me an update. I'll mark you down as working remotely. Take care.'

'Thanks.' I hung up.

Now that was out of the way, I could move on to the text messages on my phone. There were a few from clients who wanted to let me know that they had emailed me through information I'd requested for their next lot of paperwork I needed to complete. I made a note to get on to that and to reply to my clients.

I had two other messages on my phone. One from Connor and one from Brad. I read Connor's text and ignored Brad's. That man left me. I wanted to let him sweat a bit. Plus, I needed to think about what I wanted to say to him.

C: Hey Lex, I'm sorry about this morning and that I gate-crashed your house with people you didn't know. I have to go to Melbourne, but hopefully I have left your house the way you like it. I have a favour to ask. The pub I've been working at has been trashed and the owner is in hospital with a medical issue. I need someone I trust to take over the office paperwork. I've left a box on your kitchen bench, and if what you need is not in the box, I've left the keys for you to get in. I appreciate your help with all of this.

I wanted to ignore him, but that would just be stupid of me. Connor had just as much going on in his life as I did right now. I couldn't turn my back on him now that he had a job lined up for me; plus, this job would give me a chance to keep busy.

Awesome, I told myself. More extra-curricular work for me to do. But it would be something for me to sink my teeth into and take my mind off my attack and the images that played on repeat when it was just me and I was alone surrounded by silence.

I left my phone on the bed to rummage through my bag to find my keys. Lucky for me I kept my house keys separate from my apartment keys and car keys. Otherwise, I wouldn't be about to go anywhere, unless I felt the need to break into my own house. I got up from the bedroom floor and made my way out to Zach and Harley who were still seated on the lounge.

'I need a favour,' I said as I walked into the room. Zach and Harley looked at each other and then turned their attention my way and waited for the next words out of my mouth. 'As I don't have a mode of transport or am I in any way, shape or form able to drive at the moment, I need someone to take me to my house to get the box Connor has left me.'

There was silence between the three of us. I waited for someone to respond. I was all but ready to turn around and walk out of the family room and move on to Plan B when I heard. 'I'll take you.'

My other big brother. The one who always had it together. Who never faltered in anything. Zach said, 'Because if I know you well enough, Lex, you will want to keep busy now there are other things on your mind. Something I think the guitar just wouldn't cut.'

My brother did know me well and it only made me avert my eyes down to my hands as they landed on my hips. Everything that I had just been through was still raw, and I didn't want to feel this way anymore.

I felt arms wrap around me. Both Harley's and Zach's. 'He took something from me, and I don't know how to get it back,' I whispered.

'You're okay.' My brother and Harley tried to soothe my pain. If only it worked that way. 'You don't have to do this alone, and you don't have to go anywhere by yourself. Harley and I are here for you.'

'I'm scared, because he's still out there.' I sobbed on Zach's shoulder.

'But he's not here, Lexie, you're safe,' my brother whispered back to me. 'He can't hurt you now that you are here with us.'

Zach and Harley held onto me for a little longer and I wished there was someone else here to comfort my pain. But he was nowhere to be seen. I sniffled more times than I cared to count. Completely un-lady like of me, but I couldn't bring myself to care. It may be a while before I resembled my former confident, bubbly self.

Right now, all I could do was take it one moment at a time, until those moments turned into a day, and I could say I made it through the day without crying or thinking of him, the man who hurt me. To get me through those moments I knew I needed to keep myself occupied, and the only way I knew how to do that was to work.

'Please can we go now?' I asked as I took a step back.

'I'll grab my keys.'

As Zach kissed Harley goodbye, I wished to myself that there was someone to kiss me goodbye. I touched my lips and remembered he already had. I wrestled with what I felt for Brad, but did I really need to? My feelings were something I needed to think about, but I was too raw from being attacked that I wasn't ready to go there right now.

I followed Zach out to his truck and got in the passenger seat. He started it up, and I was lulled into a false sense of security the same as when I started my own car. The rumble soothed me.

The ride to my holiday house was only five minutes. Like everything in a small town, nothing was ever too far away. As Zach moved through the gears of his truck and opened up the throttle, we flew down Bayly Street. The speed, the sound, sitting next to Zach and that rushing feeling in my veins. I let out my holy shit breath I was holding with a little squeal.

'There's the Lexie Black I know, who loves the sound and feel of a V8.'

'You are going to get busted one day for driving like that.'

Zach raised the family trademark one eyebrow in my direction before he shrugged his shoulder. 'It's going to take some time for you to find what's now normal for you and maybe that involves you spending more time up here with Harley and me.'

I matched Zach's raised one eyebrow with my own before I too gave him the shrug of my shoulder. Spending more time here was something I was definitely going to have to think about.

Zach pulled into the driveway of the holiday house I owned in Mulwala. It was on the water and was once our family home. I purchased it from my parents when I couldn't stand the thought that someone else would live here.

I pulled my house keys from my pocket as I got out of Zach's truck. He took them from my palm as we reached the front door. I wasn't sure why, but he did, and I was glad.

My front door swung open and both Zach and I stood on the front step.

'I can go in and get the box if you don't want to go in,' Zach said as he turned to face me.

But I wanted to see how tidy my house really was. 'No, I want to see for myself how Connor has left the place.'

Zach turned on the first light switch he could reach, and I was surprised by what I saw. No mess. Connor didn't bullshit me when he said he had left my house just the way I liked it. I walked to the kitchen with Zach close behind me and picked up the box Connor had left then headed back for the front door. I was momentarily happy that I had something that would keep me occupied.

Six

Brad

I felt bad for the way I'd left Alex, without a proper goodbye or an explanation as to why, even though she was peacefully asleep. Somewhere deep down I knew I shouldn't have left her, especially after I kissed her lips. That was when I should have woken her up to tell her that my job had called me back to Melbourne for a new case. Apparently, I was needed, but I didn't believe that was true even for a minute.

I knew the attack on Alex had fried her nerves, knocked her around a little, and she would probably want me — but when I wasn't there to comfort her when she woke up. She would mostly likely be upset with me and possibly do something stupid. But I told myself she was safe where she was, with her brother and Harley. She was away from the jerk who squashed her confidence and bruised her face.

But like the coward I was, I took the easy way out and left while Alex slept curled up in the foetal position. I was on my way back to Melbourne. The drive back was not the same as the drive up. Alex wasn't by my side for starters. There was no hand to reach out and hold.

Why did I want her to be not too far away from me? Why did I feel this way? Alex for sure needed more time to work out if I was what she needed. For that to happen, it was best if I wasn't around – this was a truth I told myself. I needed to believe that one day I could make Alex Black mine.

So, I dragged my arse back to a legal job I told myself I didn't want to do anymore. A job where I was sure as hell I wasn't needed on this new case about to start. When I heard my message tone, I couldn't help but pull over to check my phone. I wanted to hope that Alex had texted me, but I was pretty sure it was work and the message was an update on the new case.

I stared at the screen and read what I could see of the message that had come through. Yes, it was work. I didn't open it. I went straight to the thread between Alex and me and typed out.

B: I'm sorry I have your car. Work called me back. I'm sorry I can't be there for you in your time of need, but I know you're in good hands with your brother and Harley. I'll be back with your car as soon as I can.

I waited a few minutes for a reply. There wasn't one. Would Alex ignore me for leaving her? I chose to believe Alex was focusing on her recovery. So, I pulled back out onto the road, let the rumble of the V8 soothe what I felt for Alex and continued in the direction of Melbourne. I could no longer put the drive off.

The city had come into view. I was now on the outskirts of town. All those lights were a sight to be seen. I navigated Alex's Commodore through the traffic that had started to build the closer I got to the central business district. I drove Alex's car straight to the parking that was under her apartment then pocketed her car keys. Surely Alex had a spare set of keys, and I didn't have to worry about where to leave these.

I ordered an Uber to take me across the other side of the city to my one-bedroom apartment. I had my licence but didn't see the point of owning a car when I worked a short distance from where I lived. Everything was close, and public transport or Ubers got me where I needed to go. Otherwise, my legs were my best friends. But now that I wanted a closer relationship with Alex, it was time I got myself a set of wheels. Alex's attack was a wake-up call that it wouldn't hurt to have a car, especially if I ever needed to get to her again quickly. I was thankful that night I was close enough I could run to her apartment.

When I got out of the Uber in front of my apartment building, I decided I was hungry so headed in the direction of my favourite Indian restaurant. It was only two blocks away.

My phone beeped in my pocket, and I wanted to believe that Alex had finally gotten back to me. But I didn't even have to unlock my phone to know the message wasn't from her. It was from one of my work colleagues. I ignored it. We would all know what tomorrow was about soon enough.

With my Lamb Korma and garlic naan in my hand, I walked the two blocks to my apartment. I took the lift to my floor that overlooked the city on one side and the port on the other. Opening the door, I stepped into the corporate apartment my father owned and had used as a deal sweetener to entice me to continue working for him when I finished my

Master of Law and became qualified to practise law. It was always a given that I would follow in my father's footsteps, and I'd idolised William Waters. For as long as I could remember I had worked for my father, running odd jobs as a teenager, then as an assistant to the lawyers in my father's employ as I worked my way through university.

This apartment was only meant to be a temporary living arrangement while I figured a few things out, that was what I'd told myself five years ago as a twenty-five-year-old. But I was still here, and my apartment looked like I had just moved in. *Was I finally ready to make some changes?*

I dished up half of the food and saved the rest for another day when I walked in and it was late, and I couldn't be bothered to cook for myself. Most of my days of late had turned out to be that way, and I had seen the strain it put on my parent's relationship. My father worked well into most nights and spent very little time with my mother, and I didn't want that for my relationship. But did I have the balls to get up and walk away from the only job I knew how to do? It may have been expected that I follow in my father's footsteps from a very early age, and while I was grateful for all the opportunities I had been given, now that I was thirty I wanted to explore something new.

The reason for something new was the woman I had left behind in Mulwala. Alex did something to me that I found hard to explain. She made me mushy inside, and no other woman had made me feel that way before. If Alex felt the same and gave me and a relationship a chance, I wanted to explore more of the mushiness she made me feel and get to know her and let her get to know me.

Alex always found a way to be on my mind, and she invaded almost all of my thoughts. More so since the first time we met when we went for drinks, where we both drank a little too much and ended up at my apartment. Our drinks had knocked off the edge of the long week we had been carrying, and it was just enough for both of us to let go. Our hungry kiss had led us to stripping out of our clothes before I picked Alex up and lay her down on my bed and proceeded in placing kisses all over her skin. Alex had bucked her hips as I caressed a trail of kisses from her belly button to her pubic bone.

'Alex.'

'Oh my God, don't you dare stop.'

One lick of Alex's pussy had had her hips bucking again; the second lick and I was reaching for her hips to splay my hands with a little pressure to hold her closer to me. Alex had squirmed against me, and I continued to devour this beautiful woman until I felt her muscles tighten.

'Are you ready, Alex, because seeing you come undone has made me so hard I'm not sure I'm going to last too long?'

Alex's yes had been breathy. 'Please, Brad, just fuck me.'

That was all it took to roll a condom on, and roll Alex over and pull her hips back, I'd had the perfect view of this woman from this angle. Stroking myself once before lining up I pushed inside Alex. Letting her feel me, I waited momentarily before I pulled back. But I couldn't help myself then. Alex's moans were only spurring me on as I pumped my hips in and out.

Alex's breathy words had told me she was close, and just like I said, I hadn't lasted long. When Alex's pussy tightened around me as she came, she pulled me to the edge of my bliss then pushed me over it.

As I sat on the lounge in this minimally furnished apartment and ate my curry, I didn't bother with the TV as I reminisced about our first time together. Today had been long to say the least, and as soon as I had finished with my dinner, I planned to crash.

I hadn't really slept last night on the lounge at Alex's apartment as I'd wanted to be half awake if she tried to sneak out on me. Then there was the drive up and back, and on a good run, one way was three hours. If traffic was a little slow then it took three and a half hours.

So here I was with droopy eyes, about to fall asleep in my dinner. Closed eyes felt way too good in this moment. But I still had to clean up my dishes then stack my leftovers in the fridge. I needed to find a suit for tomorrow and pick out a shirt and tie to match. Then a shower was in order, because with God as my witness, there was an awful smell around me now.

I showered and changed into clean black briefs, dumping my clothes, jeans and a tee-shirt in the hamper with my other dirty clothes. Washing. A job for another day when I wasn't so tired. I grabbed my phone from where I left it on the lounge, checked my alarm was set and then I headed to bed.

But sleep didn't come as easily as I hoped it would, considering how tired I was. Alex once again invaded my thoughts. If I was lucky enough tonight, I would get to dream about her too. Dream that I got to kiss her lips again, and not the softest goodbye I'd left on her lips earlier today.

No. I would dream I got to kiss her like the nights I brought her back here to my apartment. The one where she pressed her lips to mine, but I took over to leave her a little breathless. I learned that Alex liked her kisses a little rough. But what surprised me the most was how breathless Alex had left me. Now I wanted her lips all over me, not just on my mouth.

Her lips on mine every time we were together had left a promise of something more and now, I was hungry to have her.

The thought of Alex here in my apartment again had me reaching down to cup my balls and adjust my stiffening cock. I gave a gentle massage of the hard-on I now sported. Man, I had it bad for that woman.

I knew that the next time that I saw Alex, I would have to tell her how I was feeling. If she was ready and listened to what I had to say, then I would be one elated man. But if she wasn't ready, then I would have to be a patient man. Alex told me herself not to give up on her. So that was what I would do – wait for her.

Seven

Lex

If busy was what I wanted, then busy was what I got. But first it was time to make dinner. Or help at least. Harley had started scalloped potatoes, which was in the oven and smelled divine when I walked through the front door of her house. All that was left now was to make the salad and barbeque the steaks.

Now that I was Zach and Harley's temporary house guest, I had to make myself useful and not be the recluse I would be if I was left to my own devices, buried in my side hustles. While Zach fired up the barbeque, I took over from Harley and made a Greek salad. Everything was ready at the same time, so Harley served up the scalloped potatoes and Zach put a steak on each of our plates while I scooped a spoonful of salad onto everyone's plates.

Zach, Harley and I sat down at the kitchen table to eat dinner. Around mouthfuls of food, conversation started, paused and stopped.

'What's your plan, Lex?' Zach asked, cutting off a piece of his steak and putting it into his mouth.

What was my plan? Did I still want to live in Melbourne? Or did I need a change of scenery like Connor did?

When I didn't answer, Zach continued, 'You're welcome to stay as long as you like, you know that right?'

'I appreciate that and thank you for letting me show up out of the blue this morning.' I glanced from Zach to Harley. 'I guess I'm not sure what my plan is. I no longer feel safe in Melbourne and being down there I would be alone when you two and Connor are here.'

'Speaking of Connor, what's he up to now?' Harley asked me as if she was a bloodhound trying to sniff out the latest trouble, changing the subject of conversation at the same time.

'Connor has asked me to look into the paperwork from The Grand.' I felt no reason not to tell the truth.

'Is he interested in the figures?' Zach asked me. I guess Zach was just as curious as Harley.

'Connor didn't say.' I wasn't sure what Zach wanted to know.

'Does he want to make an offer? To acquire the business?' Zach fired off his questions, his tone tight. He must have thought I had all the answers. But I really didn't know what Connor was up to.

'Jesus, Zach, I don't know.' Connor didn't tell me much, so there was nothing for me to pass on. 'Connor's an employee at The Grand and if he wants to continue to be employed, someone has to pay the bills, and you know Connor has the money to do so.' I breathed in and counted to five, not happy that I was being grilled over Connor's request for my help. 'Zach, Connor just sold all of his businesses for a clean slate, so don't be so quick to jump to conclusions about what he's up to. Next time you see Connor, ask him yourself.'

'Okay.'

Silence fell around the kitchen table. I didn't want a heated discussion with Zach, and I didn't always want to have to stick up for Connor either. These two needed to sort out their differences. I finished my steak, salad and potatoes then excused myself from the table and stacked my dishes in the dishwasher with all the other dirty dishes. But I needed to wait for Zach and Harley's dishes before I could turn it on.

Time to unwind a little before I started on the box Connor left me. I grabbed the guitar I'd left on the lounge and sat down to strum a couple of chords. I was rusty. Or was I a little distracted? Maybe I was a little of both. When Harley sat down next to me, I wondered what her plan was. Was this her way to encourage me? I think I was about to find out.

'I thought maybe you could play me something?'

'Have you got a request?

'Isn't there something new you're working on?' Harley knew I wasn't shy when it came to the guitar. I did after all crash one of Zach's events with Connor by my side.

What Harley had asked me stumped me. I hadn't worked on anything new in a while. It was time to up my game and learn a new cover. Challenge accepted. This was how I got through uni. When I played the guitar, it helped take the edge off some of my stress. I guess Harley thought I needed this moment to only think about the guitar in my hand. Looking at the strings on the guitar, Harley was right, and playing it would help me be not so wound up.

When I didn't reply to Harley's question, she offered me a suggestion. 'I found a song you could sink your teeth into.' I looked over at her and saw a piece of paper in her hand. Harley had printed out lyrics and sheet music for 'Bathroom Floor' by Maddie and Tae.

I took the sheet, read it over once then said, 'Shouldn't you be the one to sing this to me?'

'You're the one who has the experience of lying on the bathroom floor. Sing it for the next person who ends up there.' God, she was good. She was out of her shell now that she and my brother were finally together.

My first run through was more than a little messy. But no one ever got it perfect on the first run. That was where the kinks got worked out and you found your own spin to put on it. I spent about an hour just strumming through the chords. Once I had the music down pat then I could work on the lyrics and my vocals, but that wouldn't be tonight. This song was going to take me longer than I thought to learn and get it just the way I liked it. I put down the guitar to come back to it later.

Now that I had un-wound a little, I was curious to see what Connor had left me. I needed to shift my focus and get lost in the figures, run some numbers. They would calm me. But first I needed to reply to both of the messages I received earlier. First to Connor. I pulled up his message and typed.

L: Thanks for the box and the paperwork. I'm about to work my way through it. I'll let you know what I find.

The other message I got earlier was from Brad. I opened his message thread and stared at the screen. What was I meant to write? I'm fine, don't worry about me? I shouldn't be too hard on Brad. He did say he would come back. Even if it was only because he had my car.

L: You left, and I fell apart. I want to say you left without goodbye, but Zach and Harley told me otherwise. I want to be mad at you, but I don't know what we are. I dreamed you kissed me but apparently that was real. If our paths cross again, I want to remember the next time your lips are on mine.

I'm worth it, the time and the trouble – I wanted to add to my message. But I didn't. Brad needed to figure that out himself. Maybe he had, and maybe it was me he was waiting on. Only time would tell.

I found the box Connor had left me on top of Zach's desk in his office. When I opened the computer and waded through the paperwork inside the box, I didn't realise I had my work cut out for me.

I wasn't sure what the owner of The Grand thought she was doing with her business. But it was a mess. A big mess. If the paperwork was in this much of a mess, then more than likely so was the business. Connor could almost be the godsend this business needed.

There was no profit and loss or balance sheet for the last two years, and no taxes had been paid either. She had employees too, so were they even getting paid correctly? Had she even paid their superannuation? Shit. Something told me that someone else did all the bookwork for the pub. But that someone hadn't been around in two years.

So now I had to go back and work my way through until every transaction had been categorised, and the profit and loss was current, before I moved on to the balance sheet to bring it up to date. Then I needed to make sure her employees were being paid correctly, and everyone's super payments were up to date. When everything was current, I would have to make sure The Grand was paying quarterly activity statements for their GST, before I submitted tax returns for the last two years. Connor didn't give me much to go on: a laptop and a few loose pieces of paper bills to be paid. I needed access to the accounting software The Grand used, and if it wasn't the same as I used, then I would be swapping over.

The laptop didn't have much detail on it either. Maybe all the owner did was pay the bills and the staff and tracked the takings she banked? It would be best if I sat down in the office at the pub and pieced together all the paperwork I needed. But someone would have to take me there and leave me there for a couple of hours, maybe the whole day.

Once I was up to date with all the statements that needed to be finalised, the office would need to be sorted out to see what bills had to be paid and what bills were still outstanding. If the pub was closed due to renovations after the mess that had been made, then I needed to bank whatever takings to help cover the shortfall. That is, if Connor was serious about his job and playing a positive roll at The Grand and if he was willing to pay for any shortfalls to keep the business from going under while there was no money coming in. Hopefully, the pub wouldn't stay closed for too long.

I was up most of the night in Zach's office in organisation mode and creating the list of things I needed to complete to bring The Grand up to date. The pub was overdue for an overhaul to say the least. I opened the website to the accounting software I used and bookmarked QuickBooks for easy access. Then I moved on to opening folders on the laptop that were solely for expenditure, then made another for the income. I opened two more folders: one for staff and the other for taxation.

A soft voice floated into the office. I automatically replied and looked up to see Harley in the doorway to the office.

'How's it going in here?'

Did Harley know I hadn't been to bed all night, and that I only took a break to have a shower not long before she went to bed? 'I've done all that I can do from here. I need to go to The Grand for more.'

'I'm about to go into the bakery for my shift. I could drop you off.'

'That would be awesome.'

'I'll make us coffee.'

I packed up the mess I had organised back into the box with the laptop on top. Grabbing the box and my handbag, I followed Harley out to her car, putting the paperwork on the back seat while Harley placed two travel mugs in her cup holders and started her car. There was no rumble in her car, and it made me wish my car were here just so I could hear that V8 sound.

I was out by the back door of The Grand Hotel within minutes, and I had the keys and my coffee in one hand, the box of paperwork in the other and my handbag over my shoulder. With my hands full, I had to put the box down to unlock and open the door. I found the office not too far from the door I had just walked through. Leaving the box on top of the desk, I took a wander around.

Most of The Grand was exactly the way I remembered it as a kid who grew up in this town. There had been renovations over the years and changes in colour, but the pub still had that family feel to it. That was until I reached the front bar. I was on the employee-only side of the bar as I looked out at the mess that had been made. I instantly felt sick that someone in this town could be callous enough to be so reckless.

I turned around and headed back to the office as I couldn't stomach the sight any longer. I took a seat at the desk and took a deep breath in. Connor wasn't wrong when he said The Grand was a mess. I knew he meant the physical mess the pub was in, but I meant the state of this office. I pulled out my phone choose a playlist and did what I did best: organised.

The office inside The Grand Hotel pub was small. There was the desk that the owner Jackie sat to work at, with a couple of chairs in front it. There were also filing cabinets and the money safe that ran down the far end of the office. The office was mostly tidy. But what worried me was the state of the filing cabinets. If nothing had been updated in two years, then I had to wonder if any of the drawers had been opened.

It took me some time, but I managed to make a little progress. I started at one end of the filing cabinets and worked my way across to the other end. I couldn't help myself. This office was long overdue to be tidied, reorganised and labelled. The filing cabinets furthest from the safe needed to be emptied to give me a starting point. The owner's desk was now covered in files. I could only do my job properly if everything was in its place, which made what I had to do easier. Because I bloody well needed to be able to find things. My job as an accountant was to concentrate on the numbers, not administration or to manage the state of the office.

I rummaged through files and found what the owner did with the last two years of bills, account statements and copies of the daily takings. Lucky for me, everything I needed to get all the business statements up to date was now all in one overflowing folder. This office was going to get an overhaul of Alex proportions. But I couldn't do that until I got all the figures to balance.

I pulled the overflowing file out and put it in the box Connor had started. The laptop weighed down the box that was now full. Now I could work on this bad boy wherever I was. That would most likely be in Zach's home office. No way was I ready to be alone just yet. Not after what had just happened to me.

Eight

Lex

I picked up my phone oblivious to what time it was and called Connor. He answered, and the first words out of my mouth to him were, 'It's a mess, Connor.'

'I know.' He thought I meant the state of the front bar.

'I mean the office.'

'Can you fix it?' he asked, hopeful that I could weave my accounting and administration magic and fix it.

'I can, but you will have to pay for it.' I wanted the green light to use Connor's money. The money he had stashed from the sale of all his businesses. He needed to pay some bills and me for my time to get everything up to date.

'You've got my account details. Get it done.' Done came out breathless. Something was wrong.

'Connor.' But he didn't answer me. All I could hear were grunts in the background. Was that Connor or someone else? 'Connor,' I said again. But there was still no answer from my brother. 'Connor,' I screamed and that was when I felt my emotions get the better of me. I willed myself to calm down but after the rigmarole I had put myself through since I had been attacked, nothing was working. There was only one person who could help me out of the state I was in now. I picked up The Grand Hotel landline and dialled the only number I had ever bothered to memorise.

'Eva Black.'

'It's Alex.' I took a quick breath in and tried once again to find composure to control myself, but I couldn't. I was too far away and couldn't help the one person who I instinctively knew needed help. Who needed my family's help.

'Honeybee.' My mum's voice was so cheerful. I wished that was how I felt in this moment, but it wasn't.

'Mum. It's Connor. Something is wrong.' All my words were said through emotions I was unable to control. My voice was wobbly, my breathing was ragged, tears welled and threatened to fall, and on top of all that I was tired and beyond the point of losing control. Not a good combination for me.

'Alex.' My name reached me faintly through the phone. But it wasn't my mother's voice I heard. It was Connor's. And before I got to speak, the line went dead like someone had stood on and smashed Connor's phone.

'Connor's hurt.' Those words come out almost normal. The calm before the storm. 'You have to find him, please Mum.' The words tumbled out of my mouth hysterically.

'Alex, calm down.' My mother tried to soothe me, but with the distance between us, her words and her tone didn't reach me. 'Did Connor say where he was?'

'No,' I whispered down the phone line. 'He's in Melbourne, somewhere.'

'It's okay, Honeybee, I will find him.' My mother in her own way tried to tell me everything would be okay.

'How?' I wanted what she was saying to be something I could hold on to.

'Your father,' my mother replied, before she gently said, 'I love you, Honeybee.'

'I'm on my way,' I told my mother, but the line between us had already gone dead.

I hung up the landline and picked up my phone but just stared at the home screen. I needed to get out of here. The job Connor had just given me would now have to wait. Everything I needed for now was in the box, and the box would have to wait until I came back. But at least now I knew what I had to do.

I called Zach and tried to remain calm, but as soon as I opened my mouth, all that came out were my sobs. My hysteria had gotten the better of me. I wasn't used to being this emotional, but it hurt so much that I wanted to break something or let go of these tears that were still threatening to fall like a river down my face.

'Lexie, is everything okay?' I heard Zach's voice through my phone.

'I need you to come and get me, please,' I managed to stutter out.

'Where are you?' I could hear the concern in Zach's voice.

'Harley dropped me off at The Grand,' I replied, just above a whisper. I knew Zach wouldn't be impressed.

'Jesus, Alex.' My brother wasn't happy to hear that I was here.

'Zach, please don't start. I don't have time for your lecture. I need to get to Melbourne.' I huffed out through my frustration.

'Alex.' My name came out sharp. Zach meant business when he used my given name. Same as every time someone used my given name. 'What they bloody hell is going on?'

'Please can you just come and get me.' I wasn't below begging at this point.

'I'll be there soon.' Zach must have heard something in my voice that told him that talking on the phone would be useless. No, Zach knew talking to me face to face would get him what he needed out of me.

It wasn't long before Zach banged on the back door of The Grand. I picked up the box that had everything in it to get the books up to date, and I carried it out to Zach's truck. Putting the box on the back seat, I got in the passenger seat next to Zach.

'You want to tell me what the hell is going on?' was the first thing my brother asked rather than the use of pleasantries.

'I called Connor this morning,' I started but didn't get far into my recollection before Zach interrupted.

'Jesus, Alex, what time was that?' Zach's frustration was a close match to mine.

I shrugged defensively then said, 'Zach, if you interrupt me, I won't ever get to the end.' And right now, I was barely holding on. I could lose it at any moment, and I wasn't sure if Zach could handle me once I lost my shit.

'Please continue.' Zach's smartarse side had come out. Every member of the Black family had one. Zach just didn't use his every often.

'I wanted to tell Connor that The Grand was a mess.'

Once again, I was interrupted.

'But we already knew that.' Zach was quick to close his mouth at the not-impressed look on my face. As much as I wanted to lose it in front of Zach, I knew I wouldn't be doing myself any favours.

'I saw the damage, Zach,' I snapped. 'What do I do for a living?' My words were narky, but I reigned it in before Zach could open his mouth or stop his truck and kick me out. 'The office was a mess, Zach. Nothing has been done in over two years.'

'Shit,' fell out of Zach's mouth.

Zach owned his own businesses. He knew what needed to be done and how often. He also had me as on his payroll to keep him on the straight and narrow.

'I tided the office as best I could, but it needs a complete overhaul. There are bills, accounts and staff that need to be paid. Then I called Connor as I need to use his money to pay for everything.'

'And Connor's okay with that?' Zach was curious as to what my answer would be.

'Connor told me to get it done, then something happened, Zach,' I whispered. Then overcome with everything that had happened up until this moment, I could feel my tears start to slowly fall down my face.

'What do you mean something happened?'

'Connor's words were breathless, and he stopped taking to me. I could hear grunts in the background, the same as when you spar with someone. I think Connor's in trouble.'

Zach pulled up to the front of his house then turned to face me, and even though our conversation had mostly revolved around Connor, Zach wasn't angry. Harley had definitely mellowed him out, and it was a good look on my brother. Maybe he had finally started to forgive Connor. If he had then I was glad. I wanted us to be a close family again.

'I called Mum too because she's closer than I am. But Zach, I don't like this so can you take me to Melbourne, please?' I asked Zach and wondered what his reply would be as he opened his front door.

'Alex, we can't just drop everything to rush to Melbourne.' I didn't expect that. Neither of us had made a move to go inside.

'You didn't just say that to me.' I didn't want to fight with Zach. 'I know you and Connor don't see eye to eye but he's our brother, Zach.' I walked past and put the box I held down on the desk in my brother's office. 'Connor's in trouble and right now he needs us.'

Fighting for control of what was happening around me, I stormed passed Zach in the doorway of his office to make my way to the room I had slept in. I wanted to pack my things and storm back out the front door. But I didn't do that. I did, however, flop myself down on to the bed and let myself feel the storm of emotions that raged around and inside of me. I cried for the state I had gotten myself into and for Connor as I wished for him to be okay. My tears streamed down my face until there was nothing left.

'I know you want to get to Connor as soon as you can,' Zach said from the doorway of my bedroom. 'But I won't leave

Harley here alone. When Harley gets home, we can make our move to Melbourne.'

I moved off the bed to hug Zach. 'Thank you,' came out as a blubbery mess. I definitely needed to pull myself together.

Nine

Brad

My phone vibrated in my pocket. Pulling it out, I looked down at the message on my phone. I stood from where I was seated in the conference room at Waters' Law Firm. As soon as I had reached my full height, I was asked to sit back down. But that wasn't going to happen.

'You will have to excuse me, but something has come up.' I didn't wait for a response, just grabbed my messenger bag and hightailed my arse out of the meeting I never wanted to attend in the first place.

Once I was alone, I tapped the home screen of my phone to see that I had new text messages and a few missed calls. The messages and missed calls were from the same person. But not the person I wanted to hear from. I read the text message I had been sent.

H: Just wanted to let you know Connor is in the hospital. I am here with the rest of Connor's family. I think you should come and get Lex.

I messaged Harley to ask which hospital. She replied, and I ordered an Uber to take me there. As I closed out of my message to Harley, I saw there was an unread message from Alex that had come in late last night, but that I didn't see or hear come in.

In the Uber, I opened the message and read what Alex wanted to tell me. She fell apart like I knew she would. But she had felt my lips on hers when I kissed her goodbye. Now I just wanted to kiss her. I didn't respond as I would see Alex soon enough. At the hospital, I made my way through with the directions I had been given.

'Alex.' The man that said her name was twice my size and scary to anyone who wasn't a part of his family. But to the woman he just pulled into his arms, he was a teddy bear. It was anyone's guess as to what he would be like towards me, the man in his daughter's life. I was about to find out.

'Dad,' my woman said into her father's shoulder.

A nurse brushed past me as I stood in the doorway to the room where Connor lay in a hospital bed. I watched on as the Black family interacted.

'Mr Black,' the nurse said. I could see she wanted Connor's attention, but she got the attention of every male in the Black family.

'Yes,' two of the three Mr Blacks answered the nurse. Connor's father and Zach.

'Of course, you aren't the only male in your family, Connor,' the nurse stated as she took in her fill of man candy that was the Black family. 'Now that Connor is awake and you have all seen him, he needs to rest. Everyone needs to leave.'

An older version of Alex leaned in to kiss Connor's forehead. Mrs Black. Alex reached for Connor's hand and squeezed his fingers. Mr Black squeezed Connor's shoulder, and it wasn't hard to see Connor wince. Mr Black pulled Alex away from Connor, and their hands untangled as her father wrapped his arm around Alex's shoulder.

'Zach,' Connor groaned into the hospital room, and Zach took a step closer. 'You're here?'

'Lex insisted. Says she couldn't stand the thought of you hurt somewhere and not being able to help you.'

'Thank you,' were words Connor barely got out.

'Take care, Connor.' The soft-spoken words came from Harley James, but I could tell the two of them had a history. Harley held Zach's hand, and that she was here to be the shoulder Zach leaned on, not someone who would comfort Connor.

Connor lay in a hospital bed, bruised and battered. Beaten within an inch of his life, worse than I had ever seen anyone beaten. Working at Waters' Law Firm for as long as I have, you were bound to see things not many people would, battered spouses were part and parcel of the job and my father's firm specialised in wills and trusts, contract and family law.

What I could see from where I stood was that Connor didn't look too good. Next to him in his hospital bed was a stranger yet to be introduced to the family. His girlfriend maybe, as she was snuggled in as close as she could get to Connor.

'Someone did a real good number on you,' the nurse said into Connor's hospital room. 'But that someone held back.'

'Not someone,' Connor answered, but he hadn't realised that not everyone had left his room. Several members of the Black family halted their exit.

'Connor,' Mr Black said. He hadn't quite reached the threshold of the hospital room; therefore, he hadn't reached me yet. 'You know who did this?' Mr Black had turned to take a step closer back towards Connor.

'If you mean the person who inflicted all this pain I'm feeling,' Connor said as machines beeped behind him. 'Then, yeah, I know.'

'Care to share?' You could tell by the way the question was asked that an answer was demanded. I never wanted to cross Mr Black as he knew exactly how to get what he wanted out of every situation. A key trait of any good interrogator. The man had to be a cop. I wondered how spot on my guess was.

'The lawyer that worked for me, Paul Christensen. I hired him to help me with the businesses I owned and made him a rich man. When I sold my businesses one by one, I no longer needed him and told him as much. But Paul thought otherwise. He was pissed I cut him off, only because he thinks I'm starting my next big adventure without him.'

Mr Black pulled out his phone to make a note of the name Connor had just mentioned.

I knew that name too. We worked in similar circles. I knew how much of an arsehole he was, and that was just how the man did business. His results had earnt him a name for himself. A reputation. I wondered if the information my father and I had on Paul would help take him down, but I wouldn't offer my information. I would wait to see if anyone would ask me. Though something told me that I was giving up the information either way.

'No,' was the pained word that slipped out of Alex's mouth, and I didn't hesitate. That was my cue to move into the hospital room to catch Alex, wrap her up in my arms and hold her close to me. Her head landed on my shoulder, but she could still see her dad. Her tears wet my suit jacket.

'Alex.' Her dad pivoted his head between his son and his daughter. 'What do you know that you haven't told me?'

Alex didn't answer her dad as shock had kicked into her system. Her body had started to shake, so I let my lips touch her skin, and Alex's stilled slightly before she pushed her sunglasses to the top of her head.

'Alex, you have black eye! What did you get messed up in?' That was her father's initial reaction, because Alex did have a pretty good shiner. But she also had a bruised cheek. 'Honeybee, what happened to your face?'

The sound of Connor's gasp was ignored as everyone's attention was now focused on Alex. She pushed away from me and turned to face her father to answer him. But she didn't let go of my hand as she explained.

'The creep stalked me from the moment we crossed paths a few weeks ago. I don't know how he knew I'm related to Connor, but he did. Maybe he thought he could get to Connor through me. He likes surprise attacks, hence the black eye. We sparred for a few minutes...' Alex continued to talk.

Did I believe she kicked out his knee – yes, had she pinned him down, maybe but I wasn't there to see it, would she bend his fingers back until they cracked? If she had enough strength to do it bloody oath she would have broken his hand.

Mr Black pulled Alex into his embrace to comfort her, then said, 'You did good, Honeybee. You remembered your training. But I will need statements from both of you.'

'He still got the jump on me, Dad. I want you to take him down hard. Or Connor to kick the shit out of him,' Alex told her father. I hoped Alex's dad did exactly that. The man in question was an arsehole in every way possible and not only for what he had done to Alex and to Connor. That was just his nature.

'I will, Honeybee,' her father told his daughter.

The nickname I was curious about. Why Honeybee, and not just honey? It was something I would have to question Alex about later when we were alone. But Mr Black was finished. He kissed the top of Alex's head then let her go. 'And Connor, don't get any ideas. Let me handle this. Don't go anywhere near this Paul guy.'

Ten

Lex

On the turn of his heel, my father left Connor's hospital room and everyone including Brad and me followed him out. Then I heard his voice fill the hospital corridor. 'I want to hear everything you know about this Paul who kicked the shit out of Connor, and I'm sure you have more than just a black eye, Alex.'

There it was, Alex instead of Honeybee. The tone of my father's voice meant business; otherwise, I was in trouble for withholding information from him. I did do the things I told everybody I had, but as always there was more the story, and I was about to give a play by play as to what happened.

'That jerk Paul got the jump on me as he pulled me around to face him, and that's when I copped his backhand to my cheek. We sparred for a few minutes, and I tried fending off his blows, but he was just too strong. I did have that prick pinned down for all of about thirty seconds after I kicked out his knee, but he overpowered me and rolled us until he had me pinned down. He landed one fist to my eye and was about to hit me again when I caught his hand and bent back his fingers back until I heard them crack. Brad was yelling my name as he came up the stairs, and I was able to push him off me and he got away.'

'I'll find him, Honeybee, don't you worry about that, and he won't be able to hurt anyone else ever again.'

Swaying on my feet from seeing Connor battered and having to relive my attack left me feeling overwhelmed. When Brad reached for my hand and entwined our fingers, I squeezed them and held onto the lifeline I'd been given. Brad pulled me closer to him, and I tucked myself under his shoulder and my hand landed on his chest. I had to admit I did fit perfectly up against him, and I couldn't help but want to be here next to him for all time.

'You're here?' I whispered into Brad's ear, surprised that he would be.

'Harley messaged me,' he confessed to me, but he probably wondered why I didn't text him myself. Truth be told, Brad had not crossed my mind as I had been too consumed in my own hysteria and worry for my brother.

'What about your new case?' I asked, like his work was more important than me and I shouldn't interrupt him.

'You are more important to me than any case I may have, new or otherwise.' Brad's words made me feel that he wanted to be here for me.

'I'm sorry,' I whispered, 'that I didn't message you.'

'I'm sorry too,' Brad whispered back. 'I left when I should have stayed.'

There was a small smile on my face; it was a way to let Brad know that I wanted him here with me. Brad leaned closer, his lips hovering over mine, and I knew he wanted to pull me closer and press my lips to his. But we both knew this wasn't the time or the place. Not with my family right in front of us.

'Alex.' My dad's voice had me turning to face him. I guess he wanted to know who had their hands on me. Brad was a stranger to them, and I could see both my parents wanted to know who had come to my rescue.

'Dad,' I said, but Brad wouldn't let me move from where I was under his arm.

'Who is your friend?' My dad stared Brad down. I watched as Brad put on his poker face. The man next to me showed no fear.

'Dad,' I huffed out, annoyed that he was creating tension with his staredown. But everyone's attention was on Harley as she too had spoken at the same time as me.

'Mr Black.' Once Harley had her future father in-law's attention as well as everyone else's, Harley stepped closer towards my father, her hand almost touching his chest, but she knew better than to actually touch him before she continued. 'Brad is the lawyer my father personally chose to execute his will and trust,' Harley told my parents, then she said, 'I trust him.'

'Mr Black.' Brad stepped forward with me still beside him and as he stuck out his hand and introduced himself. 'Brad Waters.'

For a moment I was worried my dad wouldn't shake Brad's hand, but he did — the only way my dad knew how — with a firm grip that meant he would keep an eye on Brad. I wanted to roll my eyes at his show of dominance but refrained.

'Nice to meet you,' I heard Brad say.

'Likewise.' My dad let go of Brad's hand and silence fell around us as we all stared at each other. None of the tension had eased.

It didn't go unnoticed. I saw my dad's jaw tick when Harley mentioned Brad was a lawyer. I know Brad saw it too, as he knew my dad would want to have a quiet word with him. Question if Brad knew Paul Christensen. Question Brad's intentions towards me, no doubt, while he had Brad within arm's reach. But for now, my dad was content that he had Brad's name. Always a place to start when you wanted to find someone.

My body trembled next to Brad's. Exhaustion had finally overtaken me, and I didn't want to be here anymore. I don't know how Brad knew, but he did, and he didn't hesitate to want to get me out of here when I breathed those exact words, 'Get me out of here.'

We all said goodbye not far from my brother's room and made our exit in different directions. Brad pulled me towards the street, with me still tucked under his shoulder. As we made our exit, the gorgeous man who had his arm around me ordered us an Uber. By the time we made it to the street and after a short wait, our Uber arrived, and we both climbed in.

My head landed on Brad's shoulder and my eyes closed. Even, steady breaths came for the first time since I had fallen asleep with Brad facing me. I was tired; it had been over twenty-four hours since I'd had a decent amount of sleep. After everything that had happened today, I needed a comfy bed and a security bubble that meant I wouldn't be alone. But it meant I didn't know where we were going either. I hoped we weren't headed towards my apartment. I wanted to be anywhere but there right now.

Lips touched my forehead. We must have been close to our destination. Not once did Brad interrupt our silence, he just held me a little tighter. The Uber we were in came to stop, and we both got out. I stood on the street and looked around, then up. We were surrounded by apartment buildings, and I was relieved when I realised we were at Brad's apartment.

I had been here before, the afternoon I'd met Brad was the first time. We had gone for drinks and to talk about Harley's new trust that I would now do the bookwork for. One drink had led to a few more and without any food, I had to admit I was a lightweight that night.

Brad had taken my hand and led me back to his apartment. The ride in the elevator was where I put my lips on his. He deepened our kiss, but it was me who had left him breathless and hungry for more. Once inside his apartment, our clothes quickly fell to the floor and Brad picked me up, carried me and lay me down on his bed. After cherishing me and making me come with his tongue, he flipped me over and fucked me doggy style. When my breathy words told him I was coming Brad leant over me to say, 'The way you are squeezing my cock right now, baby cakes, tells me just how hard you are going to come.'

I had never come that hard before that I felt aftershocks roll through me for the rest of the night as he lay behind me with his arm around me and semi-hard cock resting against the small of my spine. Every Friday night that followed our first time together had been the same, only I had stayed the first time and gone home every other Friday night.

I didn't trust myself enough with Brad yet, but he made me feel things I had never felt with the boyfriend I'd had throughout university. Brad would never take advantage of me, but I knew the next time we were intimately alone together, our shared one-nights together would never be enough.

I knew in the weeks I had gotten to know this man that if we spent enough time together, I would fall deep, and I didn't think that I would ever be able to come back from that. So here I was with Brad holding my hand, remembering the way he'd made me feel on the way up to his apartment all of those Friday nights.

I didn't know what was about to happen and wasn't sure if I was ready for anything to happen. I held my breath from the moment the elevator doors closed to the moment they opened on Brad's floor.

'Breathe,' Brad said straight into my ear, without volume, as we stepped off the elevator.

I inhaled one deep breath in but let it out too quickly. So, I counted to five on my next breath in, held it for five and exhaled for five. I did this the whole way to Brad's front door.

'You know every time we get to your door, we're almost ready to lose our clothes and have sex.'

Brad slid his key into the lock. 'Not tonight. If you think anything other than me laying you down and holding you tight for the rest of the night is happening, then you need to get to know me a little better.'

What Brad said calmed the place inside of me that had me starting to panic. But his words stopped me from going there, and relief washed over me.

'I'd like to spend more time together.'

'We will.'

Two hands cupped the column of my neck. Somehow, Brad knew my exhaustion had set in. His apartment door was open, and a moment later I was in his arms. One arm wrapped under my legs, and the other arm was around my back. The front door had been kicked closed and before I knew it, Brad had laid me down on his bed.

I stripped out of most of the clothes I'd put on this afternoon. Boots, jeans, jumper, tee-shirt, bra and socks. All that was left was my black lacy camisole and black lace panties. I pushed the doona and sheet down and slid in underneath. My head hit the pillow, and I willed for sleep to come. But it didn't. My eyes were still wide open.

'Talk to me.' Brad got into bed in only his track pants and lay down beside me. He turned his body to face me.

'I'm tired.' I just wanted to close my eyes and fall asleep.

'What happened today?'

'I was on the phone with Connor this morning while he lay on the concrete bruised and battered. He was here and I was so far away, and my brother needed me.'

'Baby cakes.' Brad reached out to cup my face and pull my lips closer to his. His skin touched my skin, a comfort I needed from this man in this moment – the gentlest of caresses.

'I haven't slept since you lay down next to me at my brother's house. I close my eyes, but my attack just plays on repeat. I can't get the record to stop playing.'

'Tell me something?' Brad's voice was a whisper an inch from my face.

'Okay,' I whispered back.

'Why do your parents call you Honeybee? Why not just Honey?'

'Oh my God,' I breathed out, a slight huff in my voice. I was embarrassed to give personal details about me away, but as Brad had picked up my parents' endearment, I couldn't not tell him the story. 'Why call me Honey when you can dress me up as a bee and have my photo taken. I am now and will always be their little Honeybee.'

'There's evidence you're a Honeybee?' Brad pulled me in closer to wrap his arms around me.

'Yes,' I huffed out with more effort than a moment ago. 'Of course, there's proof I'm a Honeybee.'

'If there's proof, I want to see it.' Brad smirked at me. Of course he would want to see the proof.

'Oh my God! No!' I shook my head as a small smile danced across my lips.

'I found what you've been looking for.'

I wasn't aware I had lost anything, but apparently Brad knew better.

'Did I lose something?' I asked, curious as to what Brad was on about.

'Yep,' he nodded empathically as he genuinely smiled at me this time.

'Want to let me in on your little secret?' I asked as I rested my hands on Brad's chest.

'I found your smile, it's right here.' Brad gently brushed his thumb over my bottom lip.

He closed the small distance between us and covered my lips with his again. Our lips moved in slow motion and our tongues danced to their own rhythm. I liked the way this felt. Brad had taken my mind off the last forty-eight hours of my life.

'It's going to be okay, baby cakes.'

I believed the words I was told, so much so I no longer felt I was on the verge of tears.

This time when I closed my eyes, I felt sleep drag me under. I rolled over and snuggled my back into Brad's chest. His arm wrapped across my body. My protective bubble was in place.

Eleven

Lex

I was thankful for the decent night's sleep. Not once through the darkness did I wake up in a sweat, wanting to scream because I couldn't stop what played on repeat. My attack, the punch I took to my left eye. But last night, play hadn't even been pressed.

The man who wrapped his arm around me and had lain with me all night made all that happen. He made me believe that he could be the one. Be all mine.

I woke just as Brad left the spot in the bed where he lay next to me. I don't know how he knew someone was at the front door, but that was why he wasn't still in bed with me. He was at the front door. It opened and closed, and I didn't get to hear anyone speak.

I was not meant to know that someone was at the door. I was still meant to be deeply and soundly asleep. Something told me that Brad didn't want to let on that he had company. Had my dad chosen this moment to catch up with Brad, as surely my father knew Brad was taking me home with him.

I made my way from the bedroom to the front door where I pressed my ear to the door and listened. Silence. I looked through the peep hole. Nothing. Not even when I opened the door to look up then down the hallway. There was nothing. Whatever was going on happened quickly. Like thin air, Brad had disappeared in just the clothes he had changed into – track pants.

Thinking of Brad in only his track pants and his muscular upper body stirred sensations low in my belly. Would touching myself wishing it was Brad be enough to sate me until the next time I saw him. Laying back down on his bed I pulled my limbs into frog legs and as my left hand pulled my panties aside my right hand moved through the lips of my pussy until I found just the right spot to apply pressure to my clit. As my fingers worked their magic, I replayed the times Brad had made me come with his mouth, lips, tongue and his cock. My body shook as my release hit me and even though I found orgasmic bliss, I still wanted more. The real thing, not just my recollections. I wanted Brad.

Now what was I going to do? There was no way I was going back to sleep after what I had just done. Did I stay here and wait for Brad to come back? I had a feeling Brad would be gone for a while. Longer than I was prepared to hang around for. Deep down I knew I needed to go back to my apartment and do the job Andrews and Co Accounting was paying me for. But more than doing the job I was being paid to do, I needed to work out if staying in Melbourne was what I really wanted and I needed to talk to Brad and tell him how I felt.

I was alone in a place I had been to a few times before but had only ever stay overnight once, so I used this moment to my advantage to check out what the man who lived here was like. He was a simple man with simple needs, or that was what I was led to believe. It was what was portrayed in the style of this apartment. There was more though, I knew it. I just had to find where it was hidden.

As I stood in my lacy black panties and camisole in the open-plan living area, I turned around in a circle and saw the place was styled neatly and minimally. Did this apartment reflect what the man was like, or was this apartment somewhere to stay until he got a chance to figure out what he wanted in life? I would like to hope it was the latter.

The apartment was a small one-bedroom with a dual entry bathroom, a lounge area and a kitchen with an island bench to sit at. There was nowhere to sit down to eat dinner, unlike at my apartment. I wondered if most of the meals that Brad ate were at his island bench or like last night when we ate dinner on his lounge. My guess was the lounge.

Our apartments were quite different. Mine was not minimally styled and neither was it neat. I loved my apartment, and it reflected exactly who I was. I had things in just the right places, which also meant I had things everywhere. My place was clean. My floors were vacuumed and my clothes were mostly folded and put away.

My place had two bedrooms, one I slept in and the other I'd turned into my home office. The best decision I had ever made was to work from home. I had two bathrooms, a hidden laundry, a lounge room, a kitchen and a small square kitchen table I used for every meal I ate in my apartment.

I went back to Brad's room. Even his bedroom told me nothing about him. Like he'd moved in and forgot to go shopping for a few things to liven the place up. Maybe he didn't want his place to be livened up. I passed Brad's walk-in robe and had to pause.

Stepping inside, I ran my fingers along every jacket, then back again. Only because I couldn't help myself. The man had a suit for every day of the week and then some, in every colour in the shade of grey to black.

I did like me a man in a well-tailored suit. It was a fantasy to be able to strip a man out of one. Maybe Brad would let me. Maybe I would let myself if I didn't chicken out first. The only other colour in this walk-in robe were the shirts and ties Brad wore. The wardrobe was filled with everything he needed to dress himself in a suit every day: ties, shoes, boots, belts, pants, shirts and jackets.

It made me wonder where this man kept his casual clothes – his jeans, track pants and his tee-shirts. So that was what I went in search of, a tee-shirt I could steal, take with me and wear. I opened all the drawers in the walk-in robe and found socks, boxers and white tee-shirts to wear under every business shirt.

In the one dresser at the end of the bed, I hit the jackpot. There were a couple of pairs of jeans and a couple of pairs of track pants. I worked my way up from the bottom drawer to the top. The second from the top had what I wanted in it. The tee-shirts. There were half a dozen all rolled up and either grey or black.

Brad's clothes told me that he didn't venture out much. Either because he didn't want to, or he couldn't, because something took up most of his time. My guess was he spent a lot of time at work by the number of suits in his walk-in robe.

But was it his choice to spend that much time there? Brad made me wonder. That made me miss him and it made me want him at the same time.

Now my heart played tug of war to stay, but I couldn't, I knew that, not when Brad lived so minimalistic and all I had with me was my handbag I had brought with me from Zach's, I needed to go back to my apartment I couldn't stay away forever. I closed my eyes, took a deep breath in and Eeny Meeny Miny Moed a tee-shirt. I pulled it out, pressed my nose into the fabric and inhaled Brad's scent. I knew I was a goner in that moment for this man. Shoving his tee-shirt into my handbag, I redressed into yesterday's clothes.

Thoughts of Brad rolled around my head the whole Uber ride from his apartment to mine. Brad lived close to the water. His apartment overlooked the port of Melbourne. My apartment was tucked in behind Victoria Parade. By the time I reached my apartment door, I realised my feelings for Brad weren't any clearer than when I left his place. Not for what had happened in the last forty-eight hours but because I was thinking about the calmness I felt every time Brad's skin had touched mine. I needed a man like him in my life. One who pulled me back when I was falling off the edge. Like this moment, looking down at my phone, when I saw a message from Brad.

B: Good morning, beautiful.

L: Good morning, handsome.

B: Sorry I wasn't there when you woke up this morning.

L: It's okay. I heard the door close this morning. What happened?

B: Both your dad and mine were at my front door.

L: Oh my God. Your dad showed up the same time as my dad did. Sounds like you're in for a shit day, hope they both don't give you too much of a hard time.

B: I'm in for a long day, I know that much. Your dad wants me to tell him what I can about Paul and my dad's not to happy I walked out on his meeting to come see you at the hospital.

I put my phone away after texting Brad to try and have a good day and walked up the steps towards my apartment to stand in the middle of the hallway between mine and the apartment opposite me. Before me stood a woman I had never seen before. My heckles raised, but at the sound of sobs, I let them go. I stared at the woman who had her back to me. What was her story? Was it anything like mine?

All I knew was that I couldn't leave her standing in the hallway when I could try and offer her some comfort – the same way she could potentially offer me some. So, I moved close enough for my words to be heard.

'Hey,' then I waited to see if the woman in front of me would turn around.

Twelve

Brad

I knew as soon as I opened the door that today was going to be an extra-long day. Two people stood in my doorway. My father and Alex's father, Detective Black. This would be interesting to see who wanted me the most and who was prepared to give in first. While my father stared down Detective Black, I was tempted to close the door and get back into bed with Alex.

Instead, I brought my finger to my lips, something I may regret later, and I stepped through the two gentlemen at my front door to make my way to the fire exit. I walked down one flight of stairs to the floor beneath my apartment, stepped inside the hallway and towards to the elevator to take the ride down to the ground floor.

No one spoke. My father and Preston Black were still in a stare-off, something I internally wished that my father would get over. Did my dad know Detective Black? Or vice versa. Had they crossed paths before? By the contest I was witness to, I would have to say no. These two men didn't know each other.

My dad pushed the button on the elevator. We were on our way to the basement, not the ground floor. His limousine was down there. He wasn't happy with me walking out on yesterday's meeting. And to make it worse, I wasn't even dressed for work. There was no easy way to get out of this. I would have to go with the flow and hope that it would be over soon enough. Little did I know soon enough would be longer than I wanted it to be.

'There had better be a good reason as to why you shooshed us at your front door, Mr Waters.'

Obviously, I wouldn't be getting away with that. But I still wondered if I would regret it.

Would the truth hurt? I let that thought run through my head before I opened my mouth. 'Your daughter was inside. I just hope she was still asleep.'

My hands moved up to push Preston Black's hands away, but I wasn't quick enough. I had been spun around, one hand was behind my back, and now I was pushed up against the limousine, my hand still behind my back. The glass and the metal were cold against my track pants and naked skin. Why did Preston not like my answer? It wasn't like I told the man I slept with his daughter, but he must have thought that anyway.

I caught my breath to muster enough strength to say in an even tone before I ended up with a fist to my ribs. 'Nothing happened.' I took a breath in and on my exhale I continued. 'You saw your daughter yesterday, the shape she was in. She has been through the wringer in the last forty-eight hours.' Maybe they were not the right words to say.

So, I continued with more and hoped they didn't land me that fist to my ribs. 'Alex didn't want to be alone. I took her home and watched over her while she slept.' No way was I about the say that I held Alex tight all night and fell asleep like she belonged tucked up next to me forever.

Alex's dad let me go, a sign he must have believed the words I just told him. But it didn't matter what I just said as I was pushed into the back of the limousine, where the full assault was about to happen. I was about to be caught in the middle of a shit sandwich, and I had to work out a way to get out of the middle and end up on top.

'Preston Black meet William Waters,' I said to the two men that still eyed each other. Neither of them shook the other's hand. Neither of them acknowledged each other. *Great*, I thought to myself. I fought the urge to roll my eyes and huff out my frustration.

I had worked with my father long enough to know when he did business and when he didn't. Right now, William Waters wouldn't talk any kind of business until I was dressed. Nothing would be discussed until I was in a suit. Shirt on with my tie tied and my jacket buttoned up. Whether or not Detective Black understood that would remain to be seen.

By the silence that continued in the limousine, Detective Black understood there was a certain way business was handled, and it made me wonder how much time the detective had. He must have some patience to take down the arsehole by the book who hurt his daughter and put his son in the hospital.

Detective Black was searching for information. Information he could use. Why else would he show up at my apartment? Showing up at the same time as my father, the detective had hit the jackpot. But would he get anything useful from the all-powerful William Waters? I wondered if my father knew his day wasn't about to turn out like he hoped it would. I knew mine wasn't.

The limousine stopped in the basement of the building my father owned that housed his business. Waters' Law Firm. The ride in the elevator was again quiet, just like the last thirty minutes had been as the driver navigated peak hour traffic. When we reached the floor that my father used for his law firm, I moved to change out of my track pants. The sooner I was dressed, the sooner we could get whatever this was over with.

I walked into my office followed by the two people behind me — no privacy in here. I proceeded to dress myself in the spare suit I kept in my office. As soon as I buttoned my suit jacket, my father turned to face me.

'You walked out.' His voice towards me was clipped. 'You've never done that before.'

'I know.'

My father was referring to the meeting I walked out of yesterday. The one I left to go and comfort Alex. 'Something came up.' Something had come up. Alex. She needed me, not that she would admit to that.

'Something that was more important than your next case?' I could see the anger build as my father spoke.

'Yes,' I dared to say to him. 'Being a lawyer was always your dream. So yes, something more important came up yesterday.' I knew those words would hurt my father, but it was now or never if I wanted to get out of what I had gotten myself into.

'A woman?' Were the quiet words my father had dared to ask me. 'You left to comfort a woman?' His words were the calm before the storm that was headed my way.

'I left because you didn't need me for this new case, and you know it.' I stared straight at my father as I said my words. 'I have a team, one you said I could have, to handle cases like this. I can catch up at any time, on any case, and step in if I have to.' My words were heated, and my father knew I was right.

'Your job is to be here when I ask you to be here and I want you on this case. My word is final.'

'Then I quit.' Those words fell out of my mouth, without a thought as to the consequences. My father had always wanted me to follow in his footsteps. And I had followed him, but now it was time for me to move on.

'Quit. You can't just quit. You have a case.' My father repeated the word I had just said, before he moved on to say, 'What kind of trouble have you gotten yourself into?'

Trouble. Did my father just say that to me? I was a good man. I did the right thing. Always. And my father knew that. We worked together, not closely, but for the last fifteen years if I wasn't finishing high school or studying at uni I was here running errands until I was legally allowed to practise law. 'If I were in trouble, this conversation would be happening at the nearest police station, not my office.'

My father opened his mouth to say something, but Detective Black was quicker with the words he wanted to say. 'William.' My dad's name was said in a tone to get his attention.

'Preston,' my father answered and turned his attention away from me.

'Your son is not in trouble.' My dad's eyebrow sank slightly, the only tell I knew of, that showed his relief. 'Your son is not in any illegal trouble that I know of. My daughter on the other hand is another discussion your son and I will need to have. But

I am here today because I would like to question the both of you about some information you may have on a fellow lawyer, Paul Christensen.'

Relief disappeared from my father's face as quickly as it appeared. My father knew something. Did Detective Black pick up on that tell too? Maybe he did. Maybe he didn't.

'For what reason do you wish to question us?' my father asked. He was a lawyer after all. He would always be cautious.

'A case,' Mr Black replied simply.

'You're a cop?' William was curious otherwise he wouldn't have asked such a question.

'Detective.' Mr Black took a deep breath then continued. 'And this case is personal, Mr Waters.'

'What information do you need?'

Was my father willing to help? That was what I was curious to know.

'Anything that will bring down Paul Christensen.'

Silence. That was how you knew you had been dismissed by William Waters. My father wasn't willing to help the detective with his case and as I had quit, Preston Black placed his hand around my upper arm and lead me out of my own office.

We moved towards the elevator. It would be the last time I would see this office. The only sad thing was that I wasn't leaving of my own accord. No. There was a law enforcement officer hot on my tail and a hand still on my arm.

'Where are we going?'

'Somewhere we can talk about Paul.'

The windows of the car service Detective Black had organised were just as dark looking in as they were looking out. Great. Another silent car ride or so it seemed until Detective Black spoke.

'How is Alex?' The deep gravel of Preston's voice made me look his way.

'Now that she knows that the same person who hurt her also hurt Connor, she won't want to hang around in Melbourne for too long.'

'You don't think she feels safe here anymore.'

'After her attack, Alex almost begged me to take her to Mulwala, and I insisted that she needed to rest.'

'She hasn't pushed you away and I saw how comfortable she was with you right beside her. She may like you more that she is ready to admit. Don't take advantage of her. I don't want to have to chase you down if you break her fucking heart. Be gentle with her. If you take care of her, we won't have a problem.'

Easier said than done when I kept being pulled away from Alex. I didn't even know what to say to that. Did I even reply? I had to say something to let the detective know that I had understood what he'd just told me.

'Alex chose me to call the night she was attacked by Paul Christensen. She wanted the comfort she knew I could give her. I won't promise I will treat Alex right, I will just have to show you that I can do right by Alex.'

My reply. The words I told Mr Black must have been the ones he wanted to hear for now.

In the silence between us, I reached for my phone to text Alex I was in for a long day. My father and I would always agree to disagree because we would always argue until our point was made. We were both lawyers after all. But this time he had gotten under my skin and made me angry, and I felt I had no other choice today but to quit. Right then and there. Leave because I knew I couldn't let my emotions show in this job, being emotional didn't make me a good lawyer. Then because I had quit, and because I needed to cool off. I was available to be taken away by Detective Black to talk about Paul. We had driven for what seemed like forever as we were chauffeured through morning traffic. The only sound that filled the service car was the radio the driver was listening to.

As the car came to a stop, I heard, 'Come on, we have work to do.'

Following the detective to another elevator, when the bell of the elevator rang, we were on the top floor. The office building was just out of the CBD somewhere in South Melbourne. Detective Black had put together a small team who were busy gathering information for his case.

Behind closed doors, in a small office that could have been an interrogation room, I was left alone. Maybe Alex's dad knew I needed to cool off. Pulling out my phone, I read and replied to Alex's last text.

L: *Try and have a good day.*

B: *Thanks, beautiful. I'll catch up with you later.*

In my recent unemployment status, I offered my assistance to Preston Black, and for a week I showed up at the same building in South Melbourne. There was something Detective Black wanted that only I could apparently give him. He wanted to know the inner workings of being a lawyer, and I answered numerous questions about Paul. How long had I known him? How often had we crossed paths? Did I ever know him to be violent? I realised I had become a witness to the progression of an active investigation. It was also how I found out that there was someone tailing Alex. W*ould they tail her all the way to Mulwala?*

My lips tipped into a brief smile; it was the same expression every time I had contact with Alex. From our phone calls to our text messages, our moments together were brief and in the last week I learnt that Alex had kept herself busy. She had met Morgan, her brother's girlfriend, and they had been visiting him in hospital. Alex also told me she had met the three young men staying in the apartment above hers, as their mother was also recovering in the hospital.

But there had been no sightings of Paul. No doubt he was hiding out and recuperating with a broken hand.

The latest from Alex was that she had gone to Mulwala for work, and I wondered if it was for the job she was employed to do or the side hustle she had or the reason her father and I had discussed: she didn't feel safe in Melbourne anymore.

The longest time I had spent in my apartment over the last week was when I caught a few hours' sleep, showered and changed my clothes. Staring at my king-sized bed, I thought of Alex and how she had left her imprint and her scent in my un-made bed. Though I knew she wouldn't have stayed very long the morning I was called away by my father and hers. She would have woken up alone and left as soon as she could. That was after she snooped around the apartment, I hadn't had time to show her.

A week without having Alex in my arms was too long. I needed to know for myself that my woman was okay. I craved the feel of her, and now I needed to see her. But I had to re-member that Paul, the arsehole, liked surprise attacks, so I needed to stay on my toes and pay attention to everything. No way was I about to be caught unawares.

But today as I walked through my apartment door, I ran my hand over my face, and whiskers that had grown because I had not bothered to shave this last week. I tried not to sigh at the sight of my father sitting on my lounge. I wondered if I had kept the man waiting for long.

'Son,' my father said as I walked towards him.

'Dad.'

'Somehow if I asked you to come back to the office, I realise now your answer would be no.' That was when my father stood. 'I have left your laptop on the kitchen bench, so would you consider finishing up your case notes, please.'

This was my father being civil. His tone was normal.

'Leave it with me,' were the only words that came to me.

'I don't know where you have been for the last week, but you look like shit, Brad.' My dad was never one for bullshit. 'I would appreciate if you didn't rush through your case notes.'

My lips automatically pressed together. This was not the time to start an argument with my father.

'I want those case notes by the end of the month.' My father's words made me wonder if what he had told me was a direct order. But he would get my case notes when they were ready. 'You should get some sleep, you really do look like shit, Brad.' My dad's hand cupped my shoulder, squeezed it, then let me go before he walked out.

Thirteen

Lex

The first thing I saw when the woman in front of me turned around was the tears that streamed down her face. Had she cried as many tears as me? Maybe.

'It's going to be okay.' I hoped they were the words that she wanted to hear. I didn't hesitate to reach out and offer some comfort, so wrapped my arms around the woman who had the same stature as myself.

'How do you know there's even something wrong?' I was told between sobs when she took a step away from me.

'Would you be crying if everything was fine?' I pointed out. I had cried a few tears too. Everything wasn't fine with me.

'Okay, you got me there.' A watery smile appeared on the woman's face in front of me.

'What brings you here to this apartment building?' I was curious as to what her answer would be.

'Connor,' she whispered between us. I didn't expect that answer at all.

'Connor Black?' I questioned. I wanted to be sure we were talking about the same person.

'You know him?' This woman asked me, like maybe I didn't know who this person was. I did know Connor, I just didn't know he was my neighbour until this moment.

'How do you know Connor?' the woman asked.

'Connor is my brother,' I told the stranger in front of me.

'Sister, you're Connor's sister?'

I wondered what she thought about me. *What had Connor told this woman about me?*

I nodded. 'I'm Alex Black.' I stuck my hand out for the woman in front of me to shake.

'Morgan Campbell,' she told me as she shook my hand.

'That's Connor's apartment?' I asked as I pointed to the door opposite mine. I must admit I was now a little more curious.

Morgan nodded.

The empty apartments. It made sense that we would all have one. Mum must have one too. The last empty apartment must be hers. I didn't see that as a possibility before.

'My brother's in hospital,' I said into the silence I had created.

'I know. I was there. Tucked in next to Connor while you held his hand. I stayed last night. Your mum has just dropped me off.'

I hadn't noticed anyone other than my family in Connor's room. My emotions had encapsulated me. I hadn't seen anything clearly. 'And?' I could see there was something more that Morgan didn't want to tell me.

'Your mum handed over the apartment keys and left. But I don't think I can go in there?'

'Why not?' I couldn't help but ask. But I guess she didn't want to be alone and caught up in trauma that she didn't want to drown in. I got that. That was where I was.

'It doesn't feel right to be here without Connor.'

Something I understood. Didn't I just leave Brad's for the same reason as why Morgan stood out here in the hallway.

'You don't want to be alone?'

'I don't want to be alone,' Morgan admitted. I didn't think it would be that easy for her to own up to that. But she did. Maybe I could now own up to my own truth.

'I don't want to be alone either.' My truth, and it felt good to share that.

After my attack and waking up at Zach and Harley's reaching for the bottle of bourbon, I needed the olive branch that was right in front of me.

'You can stay with me,' I offered as I turned to open my front door. But Morgan didn't follow me; she stood in the same spot.

'Do you mind if grab my things?' Morgan asked as she hooked her thumb over her shoulder.

'Sure,' I told her as she moved closer to Connor's apartment.

Morgan disappeared from sight to grab her things while I stood at my apartment door. She didn't take long to collect her things so she must not have had time to unpack anything. I opened my door and moved aside to let Morgan pass, then she followed me inside.

I showed her to the room she could sleep in. The space was set up as an office and this was where I worked when I was home. It also had a queen bed in it. Thoughts of work crossed my mind, but who was I kidding. I wouldn't be getting any work done. I would have to catch up on it another time.

Morgan put her bags down and made herself comfortable on my lounge. I'd put the television on with the sound down, but her attention was drawn to my guitar, my new black guitar. I sat down at the other end of my corner lounge and pulled my new guitar onto my lap.

I picked at the strings and moved my fingers through a few chord changes of a couple of songs I knew well. Then I remembered the sheet music Harley had given me to learn. I was always rusty when it came to a new song and needed a lot of practise. My key changes were sloppy. Connor would kick my arse if he knew how slack I had been.

Challenge accepted, I told myself. I needed to practise in the spare time I allowed myself. It would also keep me busy.

'Wow,' Morgan said as she watched me mess with my guitar.

'You play?' There was something intriguing about the woman opposite me.

'No, but I would like to,' Morgan told me. 'You make it look easy.'

'I'm a little rusty, but I could teach you.' It would be my reason to get better at my chord changes.

'I would like that.' Morgan gave me a smile that was less sad than before.

Then I remembered I still had the first guitar I'd ever bought. Connor was there that day. I put my guitar down on the lounge and got up, found my old guitar in the back of my wardrobe and brought it out for Morgan.

'Connor came with me the day I purchased this guitar,' I told Morgan as I handed it over. 'He bought a guitar that day too, and I would love you to have this.'

'Thank you,' Morgan told me as she sat the guitar on her knees and her fingers over the strings. She strummed down then up. Before Morgan could learn any song, she would have to first learn how to tune her guitar.

'Your guitar needs to be tuned, then we can find a song to learn together,' I said as I sat back down on the lounge.

'What about the last bit of the song you played?' Morgan asked.

'It's 'Bathroom Floor' by Maddie and Tae,' I replied. 'A new song I was challenged to learn.'

'I like it. It sounds catchy.'

Playing the guitar had helped me through university and the broken hearts I'd had along the way. Now playing the guitar would help me through this rough patch I seemed to have found myself in. I now had something other than work, my attack and Brad to think about. A friendship with Morgan. Being nosy also helped. I was interested and wanted to know: Did my brother have a girlfriend? One that no one knew about?

'How do you know my brother?' Never before had I seen Connor with a woman. I knew he had wooed plenty of them. But none of them had hung around long enough to be called a girlfriend. I knew all about Connor's arsehole ways, but something told me he didn't want to be one anymore.

If Morgan had been curled up next to Connor in the hospital, she was his woman. He was her man. Even if they hadn't figured that out yet. I knew it, I could just tell by the tears that ran down her face earlier.

'Your brother caught me asleep in the apartment above The Grand one night after his shift.'

What I heard was a surprise. But there was more. 'We ran into each other a few times after that, and one thing led to another and, well, here I am.'

There was a small smile on Morgan's face as she reminisced. I could tell she was happy, and my brother had made her feel that way. I was pleased for them. Both of my brothers had found love. Had I found love? The one? Who at the end of the day loved me and I loved them?

'I'm glad you found my brother,' I told Morgan honestly. 'He will be good for you, the same way you will be good for him.'

'What about you?' Morgan asked, and I gave her the signature raised eyebrow that every member of the Black family had. 'Are the bruises on your face why you don't want to be alone?'

I didn't expect that at all from Morgan. But if I got to stick my nose in, then so did she.

Okay, well here went nothing.

Nothing lost, nothing gained.

Right.

'I'm no longer invisible; being stalked and assaulted has left me feeling vulnerable. I'm rattled and I don't know how to stop this free-falling feeling I have.' I took a deep breath and tried not to let any of my emotions get the better of me.

'What happened?' I guess Morgan was curious too.

So, I simply said, 'The same person who put Connor in the hospital also attacked me. The lawyer Connor fired is the reason I have bruises on my face.'

Morgan gasped, like the words I had said weren't true. But she could see my eye and cheek had now turned purple and yellow. A sign my face had started to heal.

'You were comforted at the hospital. I caught a glimpse of the man you held on to.' Morgan had seen me, even though I hadn't seen her. I couldn't lie to her, even if I could lie to myself.

'I met that man a month or so ago through my brother Zach's girlfriend Harley. It's new. We've been hooking up on Friday nights after a few end of week drinks.'

'I'm sure you two will figure it out. The same way Connor and I will.'

I wished I could feel the confidence Morgan portrayed in the words she told me.

'I don't want to get hurt. I don't want to fall so hard I can't get back up again when they walk away because things got to be too hard.'

'You and I can't let what happened in the past turn us off the future, or we will never find our one true love.' Maybe Morgan knew something I didn't.

Was Brad my one true love? With him on my mind, I reached for my phone to send a text. Scrolling through our message thread I saw our exchange of good mornings and sleep tights. Brad checking in gave me a warm and fuzzy feeling like I was falling even harder for this man.

L: I want more than just end of week drinks and spending Friday nights with you.

B: I want to spend more time with my arms around you.

L: I'd like that.

For the better part of a week, Morgan and I got to know each other. If my brother wasn't where he was, then I may never have had this chance to get to know Morgan this well. I made the most of the time I didn't have to spend alone. It was nice to have a roommate.

I even found some time to show Morgan what I knew about guitars. She had a good ear and tuned her strings perfectly. Morgan was a quick learner. She picked up the chords and the changes easily. The woman was a natural, and I wondered if she would ever let me hear her sing more than the few words she had already sung. Maybe when we got to the words of the song we were learning, Morgan would join me with the vocals.

As Morgan had not been to Melbourne before, she needed to see the sights. I showed her a few of my favourite places that included my brother Zach's business Little Beats, a karaoke bar. I met Jaime Thomas the night we went to Little Beats. Jaime and his brothers had been staying upstairs in the apartment my mother let them borrow. Morgan invited Jaime along, as she thought it would be a good idea to meet a member of the family who had stepped in to help with their mother's business. Which reminded me there was work I still needed to do at The Grand.

I guess a trip north was on the cards in the near future.

Morgan and I also spent time with my brother in the hospital and although we visited when we were supposed to, my brother was always asleep – not surprising given the beating he'd received and the pain medication he was on. Morgan would hold Connor's hand and hum along to Sarah McLachlan's 'Angel', while I read through and responded to my work emails.

'I need a favour,' Morgan said after our last visit to the hospital to see Connor.

'Sure,' I replied, and wondered what Morgan possibly needed.

'My leave is almost up, and I need to go home and get ready for work.'

'You need a lift?' I enquired. My signature eyebrow was raised.

'Yes.' Morgan was relieved I knew what she needed. 'I know it's a big favour. Connor drove Jackie's car down, and I know Connor doesn't have a car.' Connor didn't have a car because he had sold it. I couldn't leave his woman stranded.

'We can head up tomorrow.'

'Thank you.'

As I was taking Morgan back to Mulwala, this time when I made the trip north, I wouldn't forget anything. The last couple of trips, one north and one south, had both been made hastily. But now as I made my plan, I didn't have to rush to get out of Melbourne. I just knew I didn't want to be alone. This last week had felt surreal getting to know Morgan better, and we had become friends, keeping each other busy.

'I'm sorry I don't know where this week has disappeared to,' I said as I left a voicemail message. 'I made new friends this week and I've been showing them around Melbourne in between visits to the hospital. I know we normally catch up for end of week drinks but I'm going to take Connor's girlfriend Morgan back to Mulwala and I'm going to stay for a week, maybe longer I'm not sure. I was hoping you would answer, and I would get to hear your voice, but on the flip side when you get this message, you'll get to hear my voice.'

If Brad didn't cross my mind, then it wandered off and thoughts of my attack started to play. Then I heard the words my father had said to me at the hospital, *'You remembered your training'.* I had remembered my training, it kicked in when I needed it to, but I hadn't trained in forever. I hadn't kept up with the brutal regime of staying fit and practising my self-defence techniques.

I took ten breaths in and let them out slowly. I needed to get ready. I cleared my head, my mind and let all of my thoughts go. If I was going to learn anything from my assault, it was that I needed to be better at staying alert. I wouldn't allow my attack to play on repeat. I would train instead, think about all the moves I had learnt, then I would practise them until I was exhausted and couldn't think at all.

I would spend the next week at my holiday house in Mulwala and catch up with the work I still needed to do. My fulltime job would always be demanding but when there was a moment, The Grand Hotel had to be dealt with. I needed to sort out that mess before the pub could reopen completely.

That pub could do with a fresh start, and I had a chance to make that happen. I was excited for the first time in long time at the challenge I was diving into. I knew now this was what I would spend my nights doing.

Now that tomorrow was here, I was packed and ready to go. I swung my laptop and messenger bags over my shoulder. In one hand I carried my guitar case, and the other hand carried my suitcase. I locked my apartment door behind me and made my way down to my car. Morgan followed me down the stairs and put her bags next to mine in the boot of my car. She was quiet until I started my car and pulled out of the basement car park of my apartment complex. Morgan and I then both let out an exasperated breath.

'Everything okay?' I made my way through the streets of Melbourne to the Hume freeway. Morgan seemed lost in thought.

'He's still covered in bruises,' Morgan whispered through the tears she had started to cry.

'My brother will need time to recover,' I told Morgan. 'He will be okay. I know my brother.'

'I feel bad for leaving him alone like this.'

'If I know Connor, he doesn't want to be coddled. He needs space to regain his mental and physical strength. In time he will find his way back to you.'

'Okay,' Morgan tried to tell me confidently, but that was not how it came out.

Three hours passed quickly without interruption as Morgan and I chatted like old friends do. She told me about her brother and all the arsehole things he had done to her. Her bruises had almost faded. She had fallen quiet after telling me how Lucas had left her bruised and battered on floor of her house. So, I didn't bother asking her if she wanted to be dropped at her house. I just took her straight to mine. Her brother wouldn't lay a hand on her if I could help it.

Morgan didn't protest as I pulled into my driveway, she just took herself up my stairs to what I assumed was the room Connor had been staying in. Was I surprised Morgan knew her way around. Had she been here that morning with Connor? At least she knew how much of a whirlwind I was. That was the last thought I had when my head hit my pillow.

Fourteen

Lex

I woke to the sense that someone was not only in my house, but in my room. I was alone, or I thought I was. I had heard Morgan make a start to her day, and soon she would take my car and use it to get herself to and from work. My first thought was to strike first, then scream. But I did neither. My heart beat a little too fast, and I needed to remain calm. At the sound of my name, I exhaled slowly.

'Alex.'

It was a whisper close to the edge of my bed. Bed. I was in bed. Somehow, I'd made it to my bed. I remembered I had sat down at my kitchen table after I had changed into the tee-shirt I had stolen from Brad, and sleep shorts. I had wanted to tackle Connor's financials. But it was a tangled mess that required more time to be sorted.

My head had spun as I'd stared at the mess. I was in need of a distraction, one that didn't involve any other thought. I couldn't play my guitar; it was the middle of the night. So, I did the one thing I knew would stop the spinning inside my head.

Realestate.com

My childhood home would always be a sanctuary, not just for me but for the rest of my family too. When my parents wanted to sell the family home and move to Melbourne, I didn't hesitate to put in an offer to purchase. But sitting in front of my computer scrolling through houses for sale, I wanted to find something I could call mine. Not because it had been gifted to me or because I couldn't stand the thought of someone else living there. I had found one that stuck out like a sore thumb. The beauty of what I had found was that the property was close by, here in the same little country town I grew up in – Mulwala.

Opening my eyes I stared at the silhouette in my room cursing the blackout curtains for keeping the morning light out. But I knew the voice that had spoken my name. It had been two weeks since he had lain me down in his bed, held me in his arms and told me he'd found my lost smile.

Crawling into bed behind me, I heard. 'I've missed you,' before lips kissed the side of my neck and his whiskers brushed across my exposed skin. That felt way too damn good.

Stealing my words, I rolled over to reach out my hand and feel the whiskers that covered his face. It had been a while since his last shave. I ran my fingers along the roughness then cupped the side of his face, letting the scratchiness wash over me. I brought his head closer to mine.

My lips were just a whisper from his. 'Kiss me,' I murmured.

Fingers travelled up my arm to my fingers and entwined with mine, and a shiver ran through me. My hand was pulled down and the palm of my hand was kissed. Letting my hand go, Brad brushed the pad of his thumb over my cheek. His feather-light touch sent tingling sensations through my body.

'It's not sore, the bruising has almost gone.'

The green light to devour my mouth. Pushing his fingers over the column of my neck and into my hair, Brad pulled me into him, closing the space between us. Holding our lips together for a brief moment, my fingers traced the hem of his tee-shirt in search of bare skin.

Rolling me until I was partly under him, when Brad moved his lips, so did I. This kiss. Our kiss was hungry just like our first.

'Roll that sweet body of yours over and let me hold you.' As soon as I was on my side, I felt Brad's chest against my back leaning into him he snaked his arm around my waist and his legs tangled with mine.

I hadn't meant to fall asleep wrapped up in Brad's arms, but I had and now I was awake and lost in thoughts of the sexy man who shared my bed that I didn't hear my ensuite door open. I didn't register there was another person in the same space as me until I heard, 'You're awake.'

Sitting up and leaning into the bedhead I took in my fill of the man who had wrapped a towel low around his hips. I tried not drool as my eyes moved from his wet hair down his face over his lean body. My eyes stopped briefly where his towel covered his waist before travelling back up to meet his. Brad smirked like he knew exactly how he affected me. The movement of his hand over his towel had me witnessing Brad cup his balls and readjust his hardening cock, I smirked back. 'I am now.'

My eyes moved to my bedside table to see the takeaway coffee cup. Reaching for it, I brought it up to my lips and took a sip. The liquid was still hot. The latte I sipped was perfect, but I doubt he knew what I liked. He had been to see Harley. *Damn her*, I thought. She always got it right. A touch of chocolate on top and hazelnut mixed into my milky coffee. Delicious.

'I got your voice message letting me know you were here but what I don't get is why your car isn't in your garage, Alex?'

This was a question I was caught off guard about. Did anything get past this man? Obviously not.

I wasn't surprised by what time it was, and I wanted to believe I was on my own time while I was here. But I knew I needed some time to figure out what I wanted to do, because I couldn't keep up with my full-time job and the hustle I ran on the side. As for my car, if it wasn't in the garage, Morgan had taken it to get herself to work. No way was she going anywhere without a set of wheels, in case her brother cornered her again.

'It's at the shop,' I said, just to toy with him. I finished my coffee and put the takeaway cup back on my bedside table. My car was at the shop, the new car I contemplated on purchasing, no doubt another very sexy V8 Holden Commodore that was black inside and out. But I didn't need to tell him that just yet.

'Alex.' Brad clipped out my name. Usually, I preferred that everyone I knew called me Lex. But when this man said my Christian name, it did something to me. No one had ever been able to say 'Alex' and get a reaction the way he did. I liked it probably more than I should. I liked that I was now a puddle of goo for him.

Like the first time he had said my name over the phone, my insides went mushy, and a wetness pooled in the shorts I had worn to bed. He would be the only one I would ever let me call me by my Christian name and get away with it. But damn him if he ever found out, as I would be in so much trouble.

Brad tsked and took one step forward closer to me. He toyed with me, the same as I toyed with him. I wondered where this would go, but I stayed silent, and Brad moved again closer to the bed and closer to me.

I grabbed the towel that wrapped around his waist. It fell away from him, leaving him naked before me, a gorgeous man that didn't have an ounce of fat on him, just defined body muscle.

Brad retaliated by pulling my doona off me and my legs until I was flat on the bed. The tee-shirt I was wearing had ridden up, exposing my flat stomach and pert breasts. Then he pounced, covering me with his body weight and sinking into me. Every inch of his skin that touched mine had me squirming, not to get away from him but to get closer. I wanted every muscle Brad had touching me and intensifying our moment of foreplay, leaving my desire pooling into my shorts.

His whiskers brushed my skin to torment me, while his fingers moved to tickle me, tactics that wouldn't work on me. I wasn't ticklish. Brad had clued in quickly, as I hadn't squirmed when his fingers ran over my ribs, along my bare skin. I wasn't quick enough though to realise that when I hadn't given the response Brad wanted, he tried another tactic.

His hand moved up my skin over my breast, and his touch caused sparks to fly inside of me. Brad didn't just cover my breasts with his hand, he pinched my nipple. And when the sting became too much, my body bucked up into him and the words fell from my mouth. 'Okay, you win. Connor's girlfriend Morgan has my car.'

'Why?' Brad continued with his line of questioning.

'Because it's time for me to buy a new one.' Brad didn't need to know all of the details as to why I had come to that decision.

'Alex.' Brad had found the shell of my ear before he said my name.

'Mr Waters,' I whispered in reply. I knew he preferred Brad just like I preferred Lex.

'Baby cakes.' I would never know why he wouldn't just call me Lex like everyone else. But the softness to his voice when he spoke his endearment to me made me think he wanted me.

'I don't want to talk,' I told Brad as I made eye contact. It was Brad who raised his eyebrow this time. 'I know we have to, but when you press your hips into mine, I want you inside me.'

I pushed my head off the bed and pressed my lips to Brad's and waited for him to take control and take over our kiss. Brad squeezed my side just under my breast as he pushed me back into the bed.

A kiss, a devouring of lips, teeth and tongue, was leading to something more, and I couldn't wait to get my clothes off. But Brad wouldn't move off me. He wanted to take this slow. He wanted to do this his way. He slowed our kiss down and moved his hands up my skin as he pushed the tee-shirt of his that I wore farther up my body and over my head. But Brad didn't completely remove my tee-shirt.

No. He used the bunched-up material to bind my hands above my body and away from his. Never before had our fore-play been this kind of hot. Our end of week hookups involved alcohol and were always about chasing the bliss we knew we could find with each other. But this was slow, like we were about to make love. I was so wet that my sex juice leaked out onto the shorts I had worn. I never wore underwear to bed.

Brad's lips moved over my body. He kissed, licked, sucked and nibbled on me. He tasted me in a way that had my body wanting more than I would ever be able to get enough of.

I writhed more than I thought possible and just when I couldn't take anymore, Brad used one arm to hold himself up and the other he used to find his way up under my shorts. Would he be surprised to find there was no underwear to block his way? The grin on his face, a little tell, let me know he liked that there wasn't another obstacle in his way.

Brad's fingers found my sex. He moved his fingers up, then down, through my wetness, over and over again. Would I always be this wet for this man? I could only hope so because this moment right here, right now, felt incredible. Like this was how it was meant to be. I shivered at the thought that love was about to be made; a spark of a feeling that would build up until it exploded through my entire body. This was what I wanted from sex, and a spark was what I felt when Brad pushed two fingers inside of me. It didn't take him very long to get what he wanted from me: my body to shake. I was only a little embarrassed that it hadn't taken very long for me to come. How many more times would Brad's delicious torture make me orgasm?

Did he know I was distracted by the way he pulled one of my breasts into his mouth and sucked, hard, I would say – yes. I felt a wave of aftershocks flow through my body, like my orgasm had only just begun. I never knew my body could do that, so I called out Brad's name.

He pulled my shorts down and then I was naked in front of him. His grin turned into a beautiful full smile. Brad liked what he saw. Years of martial arts lessons had helped condition my body to the way it was, and it got better every day. I was fitter, thanks to the regime I'd put myself through in the last two weeks. I was lean with muscles in all the right places.

Brad rolled the condom over his hardness, then leaned in to kiss me before he lined himself up and pushed his length into my sex. He was all the way home when I let out a deep panting breath. Brad was a lot to get used to. I knew my muscles had clamped down on his cock, and I wondered if he liked that. When oh and ah left his mouth, it gave me the feeling that he did in fact like me clamped around him. I let out my own oh and ah when I felt Brad pinch one of my nipples with his finger and thumb and the other with the bite of his teeth.

My bound hands moved over Brad's head as he brought his lips up to kiss me. His movements in and out of me became quicker. Was he close? To the edge of his bliss? After the assault on my nipples, I knew I was close to another one of mine.

My sex pulsated, and I felt muscle spasms all over me. Did I start the chain reaction that pulled Brad over the edge? Or had Brad started the chain reaction when he moaned then stilled inside of me? I wasn't too sure. We were both lost in our own bliss and far too breathless to speak.

'Alex.' Brad spoke first as he pulled out and rolled off me.

He lay on his back to come down from his own high as I rolled over to look at the man who had just sated me blissfully.

'That was amazing.' The words were whispered into the silence of my bedroom. A giggle had escaped into the silence. We both had spoken the same words.

Brad took the tee-shirt from my wrists, then he pulled me closer to him. I rested my head on his shoulder and closed my eyes. I didn't protest when Brad untangled himself from me and covered me with my doona. He had a condom to take care of, and I didn't feel the need to get out of bed just yet. I closed my eyes and let sleep, or was that bliss, overtake me.

Fifteen

Brad

After spending a week with Preston Black as he investigated Paul Christensen, while sometimes contemplating what line of work I wanted to do, I thought about Alex and how we had missed our regular end of week catch ups. It had been two weeks since I had lain my eyes on her and all I wanted to do was burn rubber just to see her.

As soon as I was able to pick up my brand-new Chevrolet Camaro, I was packing a bag and heading north. I had gotten her voice message so I knew exactly where she was, where she had escaped to. The same little country town she'd made me drive her to not that long ago.

Looking up I saw Melbourne was now in my rear-view as I made my way north. Tyres rolled on my new black Camaro. Three hours were a long time to think about Alex and me. Wanting to surprise

Alex but not startle her so she wouldn't hurt me, I texted Zach my request to pick up the spare key to Alex's house.

When I got to Mulwala, I found Alex asleep at the kitchen table. Picking her up, I laid her down in bed and watched as she snuggled into her doona. Her open laptop caught my eye. Alex had left Realestate.com open and was looking at a house. Was she serious about buying this house? It would be perfect for us. How pissed would she be if I bought this house for her? For us? Bringing the details up on my phone, I sent off an inquiry. As much as this family house was Alex's go-to when shit hit the fan, she had offered the same thing to Connor. If she was thinking about staying here permanently, she would want a house that offered an office out the front where she could run her business and lock the door and leave it all behind her at the end of the day. This house offered all of that.

I don't know how long I slept on the couch for, but I woke to movement in the house. When I went to check on Alex I knew she sensed someone in her room. Not taking any chances, I spoke her name. I wanted to surprise her, but not in a creepy way. I didn't want to startle my woman and end up with a broken hand, or worse, broken ribs. The perfect moment to tackle a face-to-face visit with Alex was to crawl into bed behind her and whisper, 'I missed you,' before placing a kiss on the side of her neck and brushing my whiskers over the same spot.

Alex rolled over to run her fingers over my whiskers before she pulled me in close, her lips whispering close to mine, 'Kiss me.'

Today I wanted to spend some time with Alex. But first we needed coffee, just the way she liked it. *How would she react to me being almost naked?* I wondered when I opened the door to her ensuite in only a towel. Alex wasted no time in stripping it off me before I made love to her. A sated Alex dreamily fell back to sleep, and I untangled myself from her and got out of her bed. I covered Alex's body with her doona and took care of the condom I had just filled. Alex had clamped down on me so tight she'd sucked out everything inside of me and now I was leaking out the bottom of the condom.

I removed the condom, tossed it and showered. I didn't want to think that Alex would get pregnant every time we had sex as we were using protection, but I had to be prepared that it might actually be the case. Thoughts ran through my head, the possibility of baby. The pitter patter of tiny feet around my ankles didn't scare me. A baby would tie me forever to Alex and there was nowhere else I would want to be. Man, I had it bad. But would Alex feel the same way if she was pregnant?

I couldn't help but stare at her as I dried and changed clothes. She had curled herself up in her bed. She was beautiful on the other side of her bliss. I brushed her cheek with the back of my hand, pushed her hair away and kissed her lips. Even when she was asleep her lips still sent me a spark of electricity.

I wasn't sure how long Alex would sleep for, but I hoped when she woke up, she would be hungry. For me. For food. And maybe for a little more of what we had just done. What we'd just shared.

When Alex opened her bedroom door, she didn't have the shorts on I had stripped off her or my tee-shirt I'd used to bind her hands above her head. Now she wore her robe, and I wondered if she was naked underneath. She was so sexy still half asleep. I smiled at how gorgeous Alex was and hoped she would let me open her robe to find out if she was actually naked.

'I hope you're hungry.' I met Alex at her bedroom door where I softly kissed her lips and placed in her hands another coffee, the second coffee I had purchased from Sweet's, Harley James' bakery. Harley knew exactly how Alex liked her coffee.

I handed a plate over to Alex and watched as she dished up a little bit of everything and took herself and her plate outside to sit down at her outdoor setting. Alex pulled in her chair and looked out over the river. I dished up a little bit of everything, just like Alex, and joined her outside.

This woman in front of me was independent, and I appreciated her for it. What we had was new, trying to figure out being together while maintaining our own space. Our relationship was more than just a fooling around getting to know each other friendship as we had taken the next step and made love. I just hoped in the end when everything was said and done, when Paul had been dealt with and I had figured out what I would do next, that Alex would still want me and want to give us a chance. Because I wanted the chance to tell her I loved her and would spend the rest of my life with her wherever that would be. Though I knew that was here in Mulwala not in Melbourne. I just needed some time to put my plan in place.

'I've missed catching up with you at the end of the week, not because of where we ended up but because we met for drinks and to talk about all that had happened during the week. I missed seeing you, talking to you and ending up in your bed.' Alex turned to face me. Our eyes locked as she continued her honesty. 'I don't know what you and I are. Will we last forever or just for now? It's hard to say. I like the way you make me feel, and I want to figure out a way to be together. As much as I love living in Melbourne, after what Paul has done to Connor and me, I want to settle down here more than ever.'

Alex's honesty played on my mind as I watched her stand and take her plate inside. Still searching for the right words to say, I knew my actions would be louder than my words and I needed Alex to feel me. The same way she felt me when I was inside of her.

So, I picked up my plate and followed her inside. She stood in her kitchen and stared out the window above the sink. I placed my plate on top of hers, pushed my body into Alex's and trapped her against the kitchen bench.

'From the first time you kissed me, I knew I wanted more of you, Alex Black.' That was my truth. 'This morning was just a taste of all the love I want to make with you, and it's not over even if one of us walks out that door, because we're not figuring this all out today, that is going to take some time.' With every word I said I moved closer to the shell of her ear and whispered, 'But I want everything you will let me have.'

I turned Alex around to face me, her body still trapped against mine. Her raised eyebrow questioned the words I had just said, and I moved my hands up to cup her face. My lips kissed the tip of her nose then her forehead, and the pads of my thumbs gently brushed over her cheek bones.

'I'm going to run a couple of errands because I know you have work to do.' Alex pulled my hands away from her face, but before I stepped back, I lifted her chin until her eyes met mine. 'I'll be back in a few hours, Alex.'

I watched as she nodded her okay before I turned to walk out. I saw what was behind her beautiful brown eyes. She was looking for the words I was not ready to say. As soon as I was ready to say them, I was going to take that chance and tell Alex. She was the woman for me. The one woman I wanted for the rest of my life. But right now, I had errands to take care of. A future to plan, in a hope that it would work out in my favour, because I wanted Alex to feel the way I did. I wanted her to stay by my side.

Sixteen

Lex

Standing at the kitchen sink, I watched as Brad left to run his errands. He had shown up out of the blue and surprised me with amazing sex and coffee just the way I liked it. He was making an effort to spend the day with me, and I had gone and made it weird by confessing I loved him without actually saying the words.

The best way I processed anything was to throw myself into something that would keep me busy. I showered and dressed in clothes I could walk in. Without my car, my legs were my mode of transport. I needed to go back to The Grand, back to the office and the mess that waited for me. I had made a mess in order to organise everything. With my handbag over my shoulder, I locked my front door and set out on my way.

'Looks like a bomb has gone off in here,' I heard from the doorway of the pub office.

My hand flew to my chest as I turned around to see Jaime Thomas grin my way. Cheeky shit enjoyed scaring the wits out of me. 'Jesus, Jaime, how long have you been here?'

'Just opened the back door. Not surprised you didn't hear me! Your music is quite loud.'

'A distraction always helps when an overhaul is needed,' I confessed my need for something loud. The music also helped to drown out the words I had told Brad over breakfast this morning.

'How about some lunch?' Jaime asked.

'Are you cooking?' I wanted to know what I would get before I said yes.

'I make a mean Caesar salad,' Jaime said.

'You're on. I'll be out in twenty.'

'No pressure.'

I smiled and agreed. 'No pressure.'

My overhaul of The Grand Hotel office was almost complete. Everything from staff files, taxation reports and suppliers all had a place in the filing cabinets along the side wall. The office now looked less like a bomb had gone off, and all that was left was the last filing cabinet, four drawers where the bills would be filed.

Before I even tackled the paperwork that was still on the desk, I made my way to the bistro where I saw Jaime put the final sprinkle of parmesan cheese on our salads. 'That is one mean Caesar salad, and you've added in a twist,' I said on my approach. My lunch looked amazing.

Jaime laughed. He was happy someone was impressed with his culinary skills. 'This has always been what I wanted to do. Make dishes like these.'

'You don't do that here? Why not?' I asked as I followed Jaime over to a table. Two bottles of water waited for us with our cutlery. Jaime had chosen a table that overlooked the beer garden.

'My dad passed away and my mum wanted me to help her with the bar. I tried for twelve months but the crowd was too rowdy, and I was miserable. All I wanted to do was to work my way up in the kitchen. So, I quit about twelve months ago. Moved to Benalla and pursued my dream.'

I poured the salad dressing over my salad before I offered my condolences. 'I'm sorry to hear about your dad.' With a small smile I complimented my chef. 'Your Caesar salad with a twist is delicious. Maybe you could talk to your mum, ask to manage the kitchen. I know Connor's been managing the bar.'

'My mother fired Connor. Maybe you could talk some sense into her. Tell her she needs someone like Connor in her corner, then you could mention a job in the kitchen for me.'

'Jaime, I have my work cut out for me just to convince your mother to hire me as her accountant before I go telling her who else she needs to hire or rehire, for that matter.'

'You're right. My mum would kick my arse if I blindsided her.'

'Well, maybe you just have to prove to your mum you're going to stick around, and maybe everything will just fall into place.'

'Thanks, Lex.'

'You're welcome.'

Jaime and I finished our lunch in companionable silence. Jaime stood and took both of our plates back to the kitchen. I made my way back to the office, bottle of water in hand. I needed to finish what I'd started in the office before I could run numbers with the mess that was spread across the table in my kitchen. I smiled to myself, happy with how orderly the office now looked. My smile fell away when I opened the two drawers on the righthand side of the desk. As soon as I opened them, I had to close them again.

Fuck, I thought, but maybe I had said it out loud.

'Everything okay?' Jaime asked as he passed by.

'Yeah, I thought so, until I opened these.' I pointed to the drawers beside me.

'Yeah, that's where Mum would put everything before my dad would take it out and file it away properly.' Jaime moved closer to look inside the drawer. 'I guess there hasn't been anyone since my dad to file that.'

'Shit, when was the last time this drawer was completely emptied?' All Jaime could do was shrug his shoulder.

It had been a while since I had gone this far to organise someone's paperwork let alone someone's entire office. But I made light work of what had been placed in the two desk drawers. If this really was the last two years' worth of paperwork, it was most likely that I would need it to do what I did best: categorise transactions. So, I scooped it all up into a file to take with me, then pulled from my handbag a folded-up bag to put the files in.

The top draw was neat now and contained mostly stationery. Pens and notepads. Post-it notes and black markers. The bottom drawer, now that I had taken out the mess, was empty.

It was the perfect place for my miscellaneous files. I grabbed them off the top of the filing cabinet and filed them away.

I would have to pull an all-nighter to get to the bottom of what was still outstanding. But I was up for a challenge as long as Brad wasn't at my house when I got there. I would still need my music as a distraction to sort through everything. Then I would need quiet while I ran the numbers, paid the bills and stuck my nose again into Connor's finances.

I yelled out my goodbye to Jaime as I walked out the back-door with my handbag over my shoulder, the pub keys in one hand and pub paperwork in the other.

Seventeen

Lex

As soon as I opened my front door, I knew someone had been here. Zach. I slid the two bags I carried onto my lounge next to my bags that my brother had dropped off. Then I went to look inside the box that now sat on the island bench in my kitchen. Everything that I had laid out at Zach's house was now safely packed inside the box.

Everything I needed to get The Grand Hotel up to date was now within my reach. The more I sorted through what was in the box and what I brought home from the pub, the more I realised I had to deal with Connor's finances. There were bills here that needed to be paid yesterday and there was a pay run still to be done.

Connor told me he'd sold them all. I tapped a few keys on my laptop and logged on to Connor's account. The first thing I found when I opened his account was that money had come and gone from Connor's primary account. I knew how much money was in that account before and after I'd started to balance out his investments. I was the one, after all, who had taken out a majority of the money to invest it.

I scrolled through Connor's primary account and followed the money to find it had paid for bills. Bills for a business that Connor told me he had sold over a month ago. *Bloody hell, Connor.* And worse still, there had been no deposits in over a month. The business had lost money, and it would keep losing money until Connor stepped in to fix it.

As if I didn't have enough to do already, now I had to deal with this and stop the haemorrhage before it was too late. It wasn't like I could help myself either; I was a sucker who liked a challenge. I now had to manage the left-over money so there was enough for both businesses. And I hoped that Connor didn't need any of his money for any of his personal expenses.

'Holy shit,' I'd said to myself the first time I'd taken a sneak peek at Connor's money. There had been an eye-watering amount of money in his bank account – large deposits a couple of months ago from the sale of all his businesses. My brother was a millionaire. A couple of smaller deposits more recently from profits and plenty of debts to pay for shit that should have been squared away.

Connor's business needed an overhaul, with new staff and a new accountant. But that was for Connor to sort out. This was what Connor got for not keeping me in the loop about The Groove. I guess a trip back to Melbourne was now on the cards. Not to just grill Connor over The Groove, but to pull and twist his ear over his lack of business judgement. He needed to keep a better eye on this shit. His shit.

I knew Connor hadn't kept close enough attention on The Groove like he should have, like Zach did with Little Beats. I needed to check in with Connor, as I hadn't since he'd left hospital. The next time I talked to my brother, I would have to tell him what I'd found. But because he'd kept The Groove a secret from me, I was in no rush to reach out. I still needed to finish up the books for The Grand Hotel before Jaime's mum got out of hospital.

No longer wanting to think about Connor, his finances or The Grand, I closed my laptop. I had kept my focus while at the pub earlier, but now that I was sitting at the kitchen table of my holiday house my focus had waned. My thoughts were drifting off to Brad and what we had done this morning. *What I'd do for round two.* Brad and I weren't fooling around, our morning sex was unlike our Friday night hookups. It was more. It was everything I wanted. Because I wanted more than one evening with Brad, I wanted every evening with him, but I also wanted him to want every evening with me too.

As if magically wanting him to appear, I felt his hands gently massage my shoulders. Standing and spinning to face Brad, I whispered, 'Kiss me.'

But Brad didn't kiss me, instead he picked me up with my arms around his neck and my legs around his waist. Brad carried me to my bed, pulled down the covers and lay me down. Stripping me out of my clothes until all that was left was my lacy singlet and panties, Brad kissed my exposed skin. My bare arms and legs, my neck, but not my lips. He was teasing me, and I was loving every minute of it. I squirmed further as Brad pushed my singlet up my body and kissed more of the skin he exposed.

'Tell me you want me to stop?'

'Never.'

My singlet disappeared over my breasts and off my arms, and Brad's mouth aimed for one pink nipple, closing his mouth around me. I placed my hands over the sides of his face. I needed, wanted to be closer to this man. Pushing his weight into me as he swapped breasts had me bucking my hips as his hard cock pulsed against me.

'Brad, I need you.'

Making light work of his clothes and my panties before rolling on a condom, Brad continued to kiss my exposed skin as he lined himself up and pushed inside me. Wrapping my legs around Brad's, he moved his hands over mine and pushed them over my head. Then his hips moved out then in, out then in, in a rhythm over and over until we both fell over the edge of our bliss.

Lying face to face with only an inch of space separating us, Brad's lips moved to cover mine. Finally, he was kissing me. Our lips pressed together and stayed that way for more than a few moments. Then Brad lips moved, and I followed his lead. Our tongues danced and Brad's lips never left mine.

'Sleep, baby cakes,' Brad told me before he rolled over.

I moved closer, snuggled my front into his back and wrapped my arm around his waist. I pressed my lips to his shoulder and thought this was where I wanted to be: with my arms around this man. Or his arms around me.

I felt the moment Brad made a move to get out of my bed, but I reached for him this time. My hand covered his forearm. I didn't want him to ever leave me without saying goodbye or giving me a kiss.

'I need to get back to Melbourne.' Brad's words were a whisper between us.

'I'm coming with you.' I sat up and wrapped my arms around my doona to keep the warmth in.

'Alex,' he clipped.

'Don't Alex me,' I clipped back. Annoyance boiled inside.

'Please stay here,' Brad said.

'No.' I tried as hard as I could to stay as calm as possible. But my voice was too loud. 'As much as I want to, there are things I need to take care of in Melbourne, and I'm not leaving Morgan here without a car.'

'Alex.' Brad said again, softer this time as he paced my bedroom. He didn't want me to go back to Melbourne and it made me wonder why.

'I want to see Connor.' My brother had some explaining to do, and I had a business to work on, and it was going to be easier to do it in Melbourne.

'Fine. Get dressed, we leave in five.' I got why Brad wanted me to stay as I was safer here. But there were things I needed to do that I couldn't do here in Mulwala.

I got up, found jeans and a jumper and got dressed. Pulled on my boots and grabbed my handbag from the lounge room. I was almost ready to go. I just needed one more thing: my work laptop. I opened my handbag and dropped it inside.

Time for a change.

I followed Brad out of my house and locked my front door. Kept my 'mother-freaking Camaro' comment to myself, and Brad opened the passenger door for me. Waiting for Brad to start his car, if the colour didn't talk to me then the sound of the car did. Brad's was as bad as my brother's, or was it really me? I liked my cars black and noisy. The noise of the V8 put me instantly into a protective bubble.

If I wasn't right where I was heading to Melbourne with Brad, I would have found a way to get to there that didn't involve a car because there was no way I was leaving Morgan without one. My car looked good on her, and she needed it more than me. Me, on the other hand was glad to be a passenger in the 'mother-freaking Camaro' Brad owned.

Eighteen

Brad

I should have known when Alex told me her car was at the shop that she was in the market for a new car. My woman was making changes in her life, plans to live here in southern New South Wales. Staring out the corner of my eye at Alex's profile, I grinned like a fool knowing our plans for our change of scenery would align because I wasn't letting her out of my sight with Paul still out there.

In truth I was headed back to Melbourne as I had contacted my bank and had to make an appointment to sort out my finances, but I also needed to finish up my case notes. As soon as there was nothing tying me to Melbourne, Alex was going to have to get used to me being in her life every day because there would be no more once a week hookups.

Alex would never admit to the small gasp that left her mouth when I started and revved the engine of my car. I knew how much she loved the sound of a V8; it was one of the reasons I purchased this car. She looked good sitting next to me like she belonged. I had wanted her to stay but knew Alex wouldn't avoid Melbourne forever; she needed to make her peace.

Not long into our journey south, I pulled into a Truckstop for breakfast. I got out, but Alex didn't follow me. I needed to stretch my legs, use the restroom and burn off some of whatever this was between us because how Alex was making me feel was new to me.

Alex made no move to get out of my car, while I ordered toasted sandwiches and purchased waters and coffee just the way my woman liked hers. Alex stared out the windscreen and didn't even see me coming. I placed the toasted sandwiches along with two hot coffees on the roof of my car opened her door to lean over to drop the bottles of water into the cup holders beside her.

'Jesus Christ, Brad,' Alex huffed out me. 'You scared me.'

Retreating back, I crouched down and levelled Alex with my stare. 'Yes, I wanted you to stay in Mulwala.' Alex turned, leveling my gaze. 'But if we are going to make this work between us, we have loose ends to tidy up in Melbourne before we can settle down together.'

Reaching for me, pulling me closer Alex crashed her lips into mine and held me to her for a few moments.

'I like the sound of that.' She breathed out at the end of our kiss.

Helping Alex out of my car, I closed the door behind her and used my key fob to lock the doors.

'Hey,' Alex said as I pulled her into my embrace.

I smirked as Alex moved to playfully hit my chest, but I grabbed her around the waist and pulled her back to me before she had the chance to give me her full force. Something told me that Alex could pack a good sucker punch if she needed too.

'I have coffee, your favourite,' I whispered into Alex's ear before I handed it over with her toasted sandwich.

I moved closer to the table and chairs provided and sat down. Alex followed me but didn't sit down next to me. She rounded the table to sit on the other side. Opposite me.

'How long are you planning on staying in Melbourne?'

'Long enough to organise a car and give work my notice.'

'Then I'm staying with you. I want to know you're safe.'

'I've seen your sparse apartment, Brad. Are you sure you want to live in my cosy, hectic apartment with me?'

'Yes. This is us figuring out being together.'

Liking the words I told her, Alex made her way to my car. Spinning her around at the passenger door, I pushed her back against the metal and trapped her there. Before Alex had time to react, my hands cupped her face. I kissed her, pushing my fingers into her long brown hair that she'd loosely tied back this morning. Our lips were pressed together, then with the swipe of my tongue over Alex's bottom lip, she parted her lips that gave me access to the inside of her mouth. My thumbs pushed her jaw up as our tongues danced. Did she feel me hardening against her? Pushing my hips in hers, I wanted her to feel me. I was crazy about her, but not too crazy to spin her around pull down her jeans and fuck her right here. I would have my way with her later.

My hands were still in her hair, and my fingers tightened as she squirmed under me. 'Baby cakes, if I wasn't so crazy about you, I wouldn't be this hard right now.'

'You grinding against me is making me wet. I'm glad you didn't give up on me.'

'You, baby cakes, are mine.' Now I was emotional as I admitted to Alex what she meant to me. But 'I love you' wasn't what came out. Those words needed a moment that was better than this one before I could tell her.

Alex didn't react to the claim I placed on her. Had she heard the words I had said? Maybe she didn't want to push this moment any further. She had expressed her feelings yesterday. Maybe this moment and the words I told her were what she needed to hear from me. Hopefully, my words would be enough until I could say those three little words to her.

Alex didn't hesitate when I let go of her, she turned, opened her door and got in. I smiled as Alex brought her fingertips to her lips. She still felt the same tingles I did against her lips.

After settling into cruise control, Alex pulled her phone from her handbag to make a call. We had talked over breakfast, said what we needed to say to each other. Her phone call would fill this car with her sweet voice and that was better than listening to the sound of my own.

'You want to tell me why you are still paying bills at The Groove?' Alex had called her brother. No greeting, all business. 'You told me you sold everything?'

I couldn't hear what Connor had said, but Alex had given him a moment to speak.

'Argh, Connor. You know I can't help myself,' Alex snapped. She wasn't happy with what he had said to her. 'Do you know how much that place has lost recently?'

There was more silence before Alex spoke again.

'You can fix this, Connor.' Alex's words were said to encourage her brother.

Whatever Connor replied with made Alex smile, before she said, 'I'll meet you there. And Connor,' she added a moment later, 'you need to call Zach. He has a right to know that you didn't sell and that he lost money too.'

Alex hung up and put her phone away. That was the reason she needed to see Connor. One of the reasons she wanted to come to Melbourne.

'How much money?' I couldn't help but overhear her side of the conversation. I was curious as to what Alex was up to.

'I'm not sure. I'm not seeing enough deposits coming in to cover the bills Connor has been paying. It could be that they dumped it into the safe and left it. But whatever's going on it's enough to get me involved so I can stop what's happening before it gets worse and The Groove goes down the drain.' Alex didn't turn her head to look at me, she stared straight ahead.

'Fair enough,' I said as I continued to drive down the freeway to the outskirts of Melbourne.

I drove straight to Alex's apartment. It made no sense going to my place. I had none of the creature comforts that Alex had.

Lost in thought, I had turned off my car but hadn't made a move to get out. Alex though was ready to open her door. She pulled her door handle, handbag in her other hand. One look at me and she let the door handle, and her handbag, go. She turned to face me and leaned over the centre console to whisper in my ear. 'I'm going upstairs. You want to finish what you started at breakfast?'

Alex's words made my head turn to face her. Our noses touched and I had to wonder if Alex would still be seductive like this when I was hers and she was mine. A test. If I passed, our bond would grow stronger. If I failed, I would be on very thin ice.

Alex pressed her sweet lips into my forehead and got out of my car, her handbag over her shoulder. She closed my car door quietly and raced for the stairs that would take her up to her apartment. Alex played mouse, and I was her cat. Would she make it to her apartment door to lock me out?

I moved then. *Challenge accepted, Alex.* I grabbed my over-night bag. If Alex didn't lock me out, then I wanted a bloody hot shower. One where I hoped Alex would join me.

Her head start kept me on my toes as I raced to chase her up three flights of stairs to her apartment door. Alex was fit, something else I loved about her. She had muscles and curves I wanted to explore for the rest of my life.

Nineteen

Lex

Brad stared at me as I pushed my front door all the way open. He had taken the last step onto the landing that was the hallway of my floor. I tipped the edges of my mouth up. My game of cat and mouse was still on until Brad was in my apartment. Then all bets were off because I knew it wouldn't be long before he caught me.

I stepped away from my front door and let it close on its own.

Your move, Brad.

Would my front door close slowly enough for Brad to make it inside? I guess I would have to wait and see. I put one foot behind the other and walked backwards until I hit the short edge of my kitchen bench. I didn't take my eyes off my front door.

The door had all but closed. It was just about to latch. That was when I saw the bag. Brad's bag. He had thrown it to stop my door from closing. I pressed my fingers to my lips to hide my full smile.

With my front door slightly ajar, Brad made no hesitation to move inside my apartment. He pushed the door open, slid his bag further along the tiled floor and took two steps inside. But he didn't get to me as I never gave him a chance. I took two steps towards Brad and pounced.

I jumped in hope that two strong arms would catch me. When I felt his arms around me, I wrapped my legs around his waist. He spun me around and took half a dozen steps until he was in my bedroom. Just as I was about to kiss Brad, I felt his hands move from around me to my sides. He threw me lightly backwards onto my bed, and I let out a breathless squeal. Not because Brad had thrown me, but because he had pounced on me. Covering me with his six-foot frame and trapping me against my bed.

'Got you,' he whispered in my ear before he trailed kisses down my jaw then found my lips.

Brad kissed me breathless, like he did every time he used his tongue to lick my bottom lip and gain access to the inside of my mouth. I kissed him back, pushed for control of our kiss. But Brad's arms moved to box me in. His hands cupped my face, his thumbs pushed my jaw up and he kissed me hard. Before he moved off me, it took me a moment to realise our kiss wouldn't go anywhere.

Brad reached behind his head and pulled off his tee-shirt. 'Join me.'

I sat up but didn't move off my bed as I watched Brad strip off the top half of his clothing exposing me to the muscles this man had. There was definition in his shoulders, upper arms and chest. A light smattering of hair trailed over the ridges of his stomach to underneath the waistband of his jeans. I tried not to drool as he toed out of his shoes, unbuttoned and unzipped his jeans. But that was where the show stopped. Brad moved out of view. That was when I made mine, and I scooted to the end of the bed and undressed.

I slipped my jumper back over my head. No way was I ready to walk up to Brad and fully expose myself just yet. I had to leave something he could take off me. I stood in the doorway of my bathroom as Brad reached for the hot shower tap. My gaze fell on his naked back then lower to his muscled legs and toned arse. The man was perfect all over, he had muscles in all the right places and not an ounce of fat on him, taut but not a gym junkie. If I stepped closer, I could trace the lines of the muscles in his back with my fingertips.

'Stop staring.'

'Not staring, just fantasising.'

Brad chose that moment to turn around and face me. 'Alex.'

Busted.

'You can't lick your lips like you're hungry for me or we will never leave your apartment. You won't get to see your brother.'

Oh my God, the man's torso was as sexy as I remembered from this morning, way better than his back. He stood so confidently, but he was a little too close. I diverted my eyes down and let my heart skip a few beats as I held my breath and my bottom lip between my teeth. We had had amazing sex, but it wasn't like I got to check him out or feel him up.

'My brother can wait. I want to taste you.'

Stepping forward to kneel down, I left quick kisses over Brad's navel before lowering my head to take the length of his stiff cock into my mouth.

'Bloody hell.'

Working my head, my lips and mouth back and forth, I fell into a rhythm of sucking Brad off. Closing my fingers around his shaft my hand moved in sync with my mouth.

'I'm close.' Brad's first warning as he slid his hand through my hair and tightened, pulling me back until he fell out of my mouth, his second warning. When my hands rested on his thighs a stream of cum hit the front of my jumper.

'Arms up,' Brad whispered, and my arms automatically replied like my hands knew what my body wanted: more of this man.

Brad picked me up, then pinned me against the glass wall of my shower. He pushed the material of my jumper up my body and over my head with both of his hands, and as soon as my jumper cleared my face, Brad ravished me. One of his hands held the jumper in place above my head while his other hand gripped my hip as he used his body weight to push me back into the cold glass.

Brad's lips headed straight for my left nipple. I gasped, my body ignited, and all I wanted was this man. Any way I could get him. Brad read me like we had done this all this before. He pulled my jumper all the way off and as he brought his hand back to my body, his fingers found my other nipple. Brad pinched me hard, and my body bucked into him.

I pushed out against Brad's torso. He let my nipple go, and as my body fell back against the glass, Brad's fingers travelled over the smooth skin of my abdomen until he found my pussy.

He pushed two fingers inside of me, and my body bucked again.

This time I didn't get to fall back against the cold glass. This time I was picked up and carried into the hot shower where he continued to ravish me. Brad's fingers worked their magic as he pumped his digits in and out of me while I tried to catch my breath with water in my face and what I felt as sparks spread from the muscles of my sex to the tips of my fingers and toes.

Moaning through heavy breaths, I was close. He slowly slid down my wet body planting kisses on my skin on his way. Brad's knees had hit the shower floor. Oh. My. God. He didn't just put his lips on my sex, but when I looked down, that was where I found his mouth.

Brad's tongue had found my sensitive bundle of nerves as his fingers continued to pump in and out of my pussy. I don't know how many times Brad's name left my mouth, or when I had started to call his name. But the man didn't stop; he kept up his assault even when I felt my body explode. My body shook and my muscles spasmed around his fingers while everywhere else went limp. I had lost control and had started to fall.

Brad let go and stood up and kissed me harder than he had ever kissed me. His lust on my mouth pushed me back into bliss. I started to feel lightheaded, and it took me a few minutes to regain my senses.

I needed a break from everything this man had thrown at me. Brad held my gaze, and I didn't realise he had changed the temperature of the shower water to cold until he stepped out. I didn't change the temperature back. The water wasn't that cold, so I lathered up both face and body wash and rinsed off.

I stepped out of my shower to Brad holding my towel. He wrapped me up and placed a kiss on my forehead, his towel around his waist. I ran my towel over my body and wrung the water from my hair before I sashayed into my bedroom to find something to wear.

Dropping my towel, I pulled out my favourite black lacy G-string and pulled it on. Next my black lacy bra before I slipped on the lacy camisole that matched. I ignored Brad. I had to. If I didn't, I wouldn't be getting dressed. I would be letting Brad's hands undress me. I found my tightest black skinny jeans and pulled them on. I knew Brad wouldn't last long if he got his hands on my matching underwear. So, in the meantime I would enjoy teasing him. Did I make him weak at the knees? God as my witness, the man had just made me weak all over.

I found my jumper that hung off my shoulder and was slightly see-through. No one would see the black straps of my bra and camisole, and no one would see my jumper either, as they would be hidden under my jacket and scarf. Melbourne weather was bitter, always so damn cold. I needed to cover up, but when I stripped out of my scarf and jacket later, would Brad be able to keep his hands off me? When he saw my exposed shoulder and knew what was hidden underneath? I hoped not.

Twenty

Lex

'Connor,' I called, as I approached him. 'I thought you wanted a fresh start?' I got straight to the point and skipped right over the pleasantries. If my brother really was serious about the clean slate he'd started a few months ago, then why the hell would he keep any of his businesses, let alone The Groove?

'Hello, Alex,' Connor replied as he wrapped me up in his hug. I hated being called Alex, and my brother knew it. He used it to his advantage to irritate me. I got what I deserved though when I didn't greet him with the proper hello. 'And I'm good, thanks for asking. How's Morgan?'

'Okay. Hello,' I said as I tried to wriggle out of Connor's embrace. But Connor didn't let up that easily. 'It's good to see you're out of bed. Morgan is well. She misses you. Her brother is a bigger arsehole than you, and boy is he pissed at you for knocking him out cold. I had the pleasure of meeting him the day he smashed Morgan's phone. I may have broken the bastard's wrist for violating his DVO.'

'Jesus, Lex. Please tell me you informed Dad of your little run-in with Lucas Campbell.'

I had texted my dad to let him know what Lucas had done. 'Dad knows.'

'I hope you called the police to tell them the DVO had been violated?'

I didn't appreciate the grilling I was getting from Connor, but I got it, he was worried about Morgan. She was his woman, and he hadn't seen her since his stay in hospital.

Raising the family trademark one eyebrow, I scoffed, 'Of course I did.'

'Did you replace Morgan's phone?' Connor asked as he pulled out his phone no doubt to text Morgan that he would talk to her later.

I smirked and nodded before whispering my tease, 'You must be in love, because man, you have it bad for that woman.'

The expression on Connor's face told me that maybe I was right, but he wasn't going to discuss it with me. Connor gave me his shit-eating smirk. 'Thank you,' he said as he held me at arm's length. 'I am grateful for everything you've done for me, especially offering Morgan to stay with you. I appreciate it.'

Connor's words made me emotional. My eyes welled a little. If I wasn't careful, tears would fall down my face. I was only glad Connor didn't call me out on my watery eyes. Otherwise, I would have to kick his arse. But I had needed to hear his words.

Before Connor let me go, he dropped a bombshell on me. 'I couldn't bring myself to sell The Groove. It's the first business

Zach ever loaned me money for, and although he's been a silent partner, I want to make it work.'

'Jesus, Connor, Zach will be pissed.' I locked eyes with Connor.

'We'll find out soon enough, I guess.'

I was surprised by this. 'You called Zach?' Connor was either brave or stupid. I couldn't work out which one. I would have to wait until I saw the look on Zach's face to make an informed decision.

'He said he would meet us here. He was checking on Little Beats.' As Connor took a step back, he noticed I had brought company.

'You have a shadow,' Connor said low enough for only me to hear.

'Yeah, for three weeks now, no thanks to you,' I told Connor, but it was only to yank his chain. I had two older brothers, and I needed to be able give to and good as I got. Otherwise, I would never be able to keep up with either of them.

'What? Wait? What do you mean no thanks to me?'

So yeah, I wanted Connor to believe I could more than just yank on his chain a little bit.

'Paul Christensen. I can't believe you two worked together. He's more ruthless and a far bigger prick than you.'

'I didn't know Paul had a mean streak a mile wide; otherwise, he never would have been my confidant. How did you get tangled up with him?'

'We ran into each other one afternoon and a couple of times after that, but his behaviour became stalkerish. He would follow me home after drinks on Friday nights. After Paul's surprise attack on me, and your stay in hospital, Brad has kept his eye on me. The two of us have hung out a little bit.' I let out an exasperated breath at the end of my explanation.

'Don't tell me you don't enjoy Brad's company.'

Connor pushed my buttons the same way I pushed his. He took in the look on my face, sensed my frustration. My brother let whatever was on his mind turn over before he told me. 'You two look good together.'

I whacked Connor with my forearm to his side. *Shit*, I thought to myself as I looked at Connor's raised eyebrow. His breath was shallow. I had forgotten how battered Connor's body was and that he was still in recovery, three weeks later. But he had gone a little too far with his tease.

'Jesus, Lex,' Connor said as he tried to hide his pain.

'Can we just go inside?' I asked as I turned to make my way inside.

'Zach will be here soon,' Connor called after me and I turned back to face him. 'We wait for Zach, as what I have planned won't work without him.'

I raised my eyebrow at Connor. Did my disbelief show? Connor in return matched my raised eyebrow then nodded his head. He wasn't kidding. There was a seriousness about Connor tonight that I had never seen before.

'Would you rather I left him in the dark about this?' Connor asked me as he pointed to the neon sign that lit up the name of the business we stood out the front of.

'Point taken.'

'The sooner Zach knows about my plans for The Groove, the less likely he is to be pissed with me. If there is one thing I have learnt, it's that I have to be truthful and do things honestly and by the book.'

'Okay. It was the right thing to do. To let Zach know,' I confessed.

When Zach arrived, he shook hands with Brad, and Connor introduced himself to Brad

'I'm Connor by the way,' my brother said as he stuck his hand out for Brad to shake. 'Sorry, Lex here was rude and didn't introduce us.'

I shot Connor my death stare as Brad replied, 'Lex wants to keep us a secret but it's a bit hard when I know half of the family anyway.' Brad knew Zach and me, but Connor had been left out of the loop.

'And now you know another family member.' I whacked Brad the same as I'd whacked Connor, only Brad's whack was across the chest and not in the ribs. 'Brad's a lawyer at Waters Law Firm, and he's been helping Harley with her trust and her dad's estate.'

Connor nodded his appreciation for filling him in.

I turned to head towards the entrance of The Groove, but Brad had caught my arm and pulled me back to him. 'So rude, Alex. But you will keep. I want you as soon as possible in only your black lacy underwear,' Brad whispered before he let me go. Thank God it was dark. Brad may have just made me blush. If it wasn't uncomfortable enough to be sporting a red face, there was now a wetness pooled my G-string.

'What's the plan?' Zach asked as he faced both Connor and me.

'Well hello to you too,' Connor and I said in unison as we both bear-hugged our brother.

'Okay. Okay. Hello. Hello,' Zach said and both Connor and I let go. 'You look good, Connor. Thought you might have been bullshitting me on the phone.'

'Now that we're all here and you can see I'm getting better, we can go inside and tell the staff our plans,' Connor told Zach, Brad and me.

'And what plans are they?' Zach asked, as he was always all business. My brother did have the right to know what Connor's game plan was.

'That the three of us will co-own The Groove, and we are about to take this club in a new direction. A classy one, and the staff can either get on board or go their separate ways.'

'What do you mean, the three of us?' I asked like I had missed something. I wasn't sure what just happened. What the bloody hell was Connor on about?

'I want you brought in as a partner, Lex, and I don't want you to feel like a silent partner anymore either, Zach. I want us to do this together.'

'I'll draw up some papers if you would like to make it official,' Brad said out of the blue, and we all turned to look at him. 'That's what lawyers do,' Brad deadpanned.

Brad did have a point. We would need a contract so we wouldn't all kill each other.

'Well, I guess that's a start,' Zach threw out. He smirked. He liked the idea that Connor would be held more accountable for what happened at The Groove.

'Like you said, it's a big job and it won't happen overnight. So, it's best that we get to it.'

On the turn of Connor's heel, he walked towards the front doors and entered The Groove.

I stood off to the side with Zach and Brad and watched on as my brother spoke to all the staff that turned up for work at The Groove tonight. It was easy to see that standing in front of everyone wasn't an easy job for Connor. But he wanted to make changes, so this is what he had to do – make tough choices and execute them.

Some laughed, walked out and didn't look back. Some stayed to hear what Connor had to say and still walked away. But in the end, there were only four people left. None of The Groove staff wanted to stay on board.

So here we were on stools in front of the bar. Connor looked like he wanted to drown his sorrows in the bottom of the bottle of bourbon in front of him, something he would no doubt regret in the morning.

I leaned over the bar and reached for my own bottle of bourbon. I was right there with my brother. I needed to drown my sorrows. I now had another business on my books. Maybe the bourbon would help clarify a few things for me. Or maybe I knew what I needed to do, and all I needed was liquid courage to help me pull it off.

Twenty-one

Brad

I watched Connor and Alex as they downed two straight bourbons. Time to put a stop to the sorrows they wanted to drown in. I poured one more and put the bottle down out of reach. Alex needed to slow down, but who was I to tell her how much she could or couldn't drink? She obviously had something on her mind she needed to process and sort out.

I leaned in to turn Alex's glass upside down, but my hand didn't even reach Alex's glass. My phone had silently buzzed in my pocket. I reached for it instead. My phone stole my attention away from Alex and Connor at the bar to the unexpected message I saw pop up on my home screen.

U: Why are you out with Alex?

Unknown number. But if I had to guess, it would have to be Detective Black. I offered an honest reply. I didn't need her dad chasing me when all was said and done.

B: *Alex insisted she see Connor.*

U: *She's not safe.*

B: *She's with me and both her brothers.*

U: *Take her home.*

I guess that was an order and didn't warrant a reply. How Detective Black knew she was in Melbourne with me or that we were even out, for that matter, told me that the detective hadn't just been tailing Alex. She had been in Mulwala and hadn't needed to be followed but now that she was back in Melbourne, tailing Alex would be back on even though I wasn't going to be letting her out of my sight.

I knew Alex could handle her liquor; she had proven that the first night we met. But just one look at her now, it was easy to see that she had had enough. I moved to turn her glass upside down before Connor could think about reaching over the bar for any bottle he could get his hands on to pour more into his glass. I made it just in time.

Zach followed my lead and turned Connor's glass upside down before Connor got the idea to drink straight from the bottle and drag Alex down with him. Zach snatched the bottle from Connor's hand. Connor did himself no good drinking away the profits.

'Time to go,' Zach told both Connor and Alex, his raised eyebrow on show. A family trait all the siblings had in common with their father.

Zach cleaned up both of their messes and threw one bottle in the bin, then put the other back behind the bar.

'Come on, I'll take you all home,' Zach said as he jangled his car keys. He would never know how much of a life saver he was.

Alex and Connor groaned when the bourbon had been taken off them but smiled when they didn't have to stumble home tipsy. On the other hand, I was glad I didn't have watch my back as I followed these two siblings as they made their way home.

Connor reached for his keys to lock up The Groove, but as soon as they were out of his pocket, Zach grabbed them from his grip. He checked all the doors and made sure they were all locked then ushered us out the front door and locked up. Once he was happy everything was locked, he gave Connor back his keys and we all followed Zach to his suped-up four-door black Chevrolet truck.

Zach parked in the underground carpark of the apartment building Alex lived in. Everyone exited Zach's truck, and I was surprised when all three of them made their way to the stairs. Connor and Zach must also have apartments here.

'Too many stairs to climb. You could have parked closer to my apartment, Zach,' Alex said, then giggled. She was too cute for her own good when she drank hard liquor.

Zach sighed. 'You could have drunk less, and the stairs wouldn't be a problem.' I wanted to laugh, but Zach was right.

'But where would the fun be in that?' Connor said, hooking his arm around Alex's shoulder as they stumbled up the stairs one slow step at a time.

'No hangover in the morning,' Zach said as he smirked at me. Zach and I hadn't touched any alcohol, and I'm sure we both had our reasons.

'Nice wheels,' Zach said as he and I moved to follow Connor and Alex up the stairs. 'She must have set you back a pretty penny.'

'It was worth every penny I spent on it for the sound it makes.'

'She got to you too, hey?' Zach asked as we walked up the first flight of stairs. I must have given a blank stare, so Zach continued. 'Alex and her V8s. She has only ever driven and owned a V8. Since my dad taught her to drive, it was all she ever wanted. She wouldn't go anywhere unless she was in one. Alex sucked us all in, and we all love the same rumble she does.'

I was silent as Zach and I walked up another flight of stairs. We were still behind Alex and Connor. But only by a few stairs as they were slightly inebriated after all.

Had Alex really got to me though? I would be stupid if I believed otherwise.

This wasn't the time or the place for this discussion, and Zach was absolutely the wrong person to have this conversation with. I needed to talk to Alex, and I needed to do it soon – as soon as I found the right time to tell her about everything I was working on would be the moment I told her how I felt. But our moments together had been few and far between. Something I knew I needed to change.

'I should welcome you to the family then,' Zach said like he knew something I didn't.

'A black car with a particular rumble doesn't mean Alex and I are together, let alone in a relationship.' I tried to fend off Zach, but I knew it was a waste of both of our time.

'Keep telling yourself that. But you were the one who showed up at my house driving Alex's Commodore. You're the closest she has allowed anyone in a very long time.'

Zach and I had caught up to Connor and Alex. A reply to Zach at this point was useless unless I wanted to open a can of worms, which I didn't. So, I stayed quiet. Zach gave me something to think about, but he also made me question why Alex chose me.

I picked Alex up and carried her the rest of the way to her apartment. She handed over her keys for me to unlock her front door. If she thought I was letting go of her to put her key in the lock and turn the handle, she had another thing coming.

Alex and her brothers exchanged goodnights. Connor headed for the door opposite Alex's while Zach climbed another flight of stairs, which I assumed was to his apartment.

I pulled the key from the lock and shut Alex's apartment door. Then I carried her all the way to her bedroom and laid her down. I moved to her kitchen for a cold bottle of water and placed it on her bedside table for later. Then went in search of pain killers and found them in her bathroom drawer.

I was only gone a moment but that was long enough for Alex to end up on her bedroom floor. She had only just managed to get half undressed, pulling off her jacket and scarf and kicking off her boots. Alex now struggled with her skinny jeans; the ones I knew she put on to drive me crazy. She managed to pull one leg off, but the other leg was stuck. That was how she must have found the floor, trying to pull the other leg off.

I couldn't help but laugh before I saw my chance to help Alex undress, pulling her off-the-shoulder jumper over her head to get a better view of her sexy lingerie. God damn did this woman look sexy as fuck in the skimpy material she was wearing. Black just like her surname. Her camisole was next, leaving Alex in her bra, G-string and one leg in her jeans. Unclasping her bra and ripping away the scrap of lace covering her pussy, the family trademark one eyebrow was on show as Alex locked eyes with me. Was she turned on because I had ripped off her clothing? Well, I was about to find out. Leaning into Alex, I pushed her thighs wide, and she let out a gasp that told me she knew where this was going.

But did she know we weren't having sex? Two could play the teasing game and this was me teasing her just like she had with the lingerie she had been wearing. Placing a kiss on her pubic bone an airy 'Brad' escaped her lips, and that's when I eased two fingers into Alex's pussy. Her wetness coated my fingers as I moved them in and out. With her hands flat on the floor Alex moved to ride my fingers, but she didn't get to be in control. I palmed her lower belly to stop her from grinding around my fingers.

Alex huffed out her annoyance. 'Stop teasing me and make me come, Brad.'

Pulling my fingers out, I licked her juices from my fingers and pulled her jeans all the way off. Scooping her naked body up off the floor I laid her down on her bed.

'Brad,' Alex breathed. 'Please make me come.'

Unable to resist this woman, I stripped down to my black boxer briefs and got into bed behind her. Reaching over her abdomen, I inserted both fingers back into her wetness, pumping my digits in and out in a sporadic rhythm just to drive Alex crazy knowing she would come hard around my fingers. Holding Alex against me, skin on skin, she didn't move as I eased the pace of my pumping digits. Her muscles tightened, her body shook and her pants gave her away before she breathed, 'I came so hard I saw stars.'

Alex turned to face me, and I couldn't resist a kiss to her pink glossy lips before I covered her body with her doona.

'What did you and Zach talk about?' Even in her current state she was still curious.

'My car.' I couldn't tell her about the other stuff. I wasn't ready for that conversation tonight.

'I want to drive your car,' Alex confessed with a soft giggle. But I already knew by the gasp from this morning that she loved my car.

'I know,' I whispered back. 'I got you water and pain killers. Now sleep, you're going to need them in the morning.'

Twenty-two

Lex

I felt it as soon as I woke up. I had done this to myself and now I was sporting a headache. But I was thankful for the pain relief on my bedside table. Brad had left my bed at the crack of dawn telling me he was going back to his apartment for more clothes. With Brad gone I was here alone, but that didn't explain the noise I just heard. First, I had to deal with my dry mouth, then I would deal with noise that just came from my kitchen.

There was only one other person who had access to my apartment and that was my mother. Why she was here was anyone's guess. But she wouldn't be here unless she felt it was necessary. Or my father wanted to know I was okay given I was in Melbourne, especially after what happened to Connor. Because as far as I knew, Dad was still on the hunt for Paul. Either way I needed to get up and deal with what was about to be thrown at me.

I got out of bed and looked down at myself; I was naked. The lacy underwear I had put on for Brad, he had taken off me. I reached for my sleep shorts and singlet before slipping my robe over my shoulders. I wrapped it around me and snuggled in, then looked in the mirror. I wasn't shocked at how awful I looked, but I looked scary: my hair was a mess, and my face was blotchy. What I needed only a shower would fix, but that would have to wait until my mother was gone. I wanted to wallow around my apartment out of sight of watchful eyes while the mood I woke up in subsided.

Making my way out of my bedroom and walking down the short hall to my kitchen, the smell hit me first and then the waves of nausea followed. I breathed in shallow breaths in hope that the nausea would pass. The figure at my stove turned around at the same time I leaned into my kitchen bench.

'Honeybee.'

'Mum,' I said with as much excitement as I could muster. But it was hard. My mother hugged me, kissed my forehead, then went back to the stove. 'Thought you might like pancakes this morning.'

No one cooked me breakfast. Brad had been the only one. Normally I skipped breakfast, but I knew I shouldn't skip the most important meal of the day. Some days it was just easier to walk out with a coffee in my hand and deal with the hunger pains when lunch time rolled around. But after today and the feast that Brad had put on for me yesterday, I was going to make an effort every day to have breakfast. A feast just for me.

'Only if there is bacon.' My mother was up to something, and I needed to figure out what that was.

'Of course.' Eva Black turned to face me and flash me her pearly white smile.

There was a look on my mother's face that told me she might just be here because she was a little worried about me, the baby of the family, even though I was twenty-four. But if I knew my mother at all, she would pull every trick out of her psychology books to get me to do exactly what she wanted: talk to her.

I watched on as Eva cooked bacon and pancakes in my kitchen then I put myself to use and made both of us coffees. And not just any coffee. Lattes from my coffee machine. I even had the chocolate powder and the hazelnut syrup to add at the end. Harley had told me exactly how to make them.

I made my mother's first, and I knew she wouldn't want any of the fancy stuff I liked. But she surprised me.

'What in God's earth are you doing?' she asked me with a concerned look on her face.

'Making a latte.' I couldn't help but state the obvious.

'With chocolate powder?'

'Yes, Mum,' I said on an exasperated breath. 'I like to add in a twist.'

'Let me try some of that.' She was clearly curious as to what I was up to.

Lucky for my mother, I had only made the coffee base. My cup had a teaspoon of chocolate powder added to my coffee. I was mixing the chocolate in when she asked what I was doing. I mixed the chocolate into her cup and heated the milk up.

'Do you want the hazelnut syrup too?' I asked her as I held up the bottle of syrup.

'I want what you're having.' She was in for a surprise when she took her first sip.

I poured in the milk then drizzled the hazelnut over the top. I handed my mother her cup and watched as she took her first sip. Her expression never changed. Did that mean that she liked the concoction, or not?

'Damn,' she said as she smacked her lips together. Her smile grew on her face.

'I know,' I said as I nodded my head, then took a sip from my own coffee cup. 'Harley has been experimenting with flavours at the bakery. I just happened to be there the day she was trialling this one. Harley gets me to try all her experiments, but the hazelnut one is by far the best.' The hot liquid made its way to my stomach. I just hoped it would stay there and not come back up.

'This is good, Alex.'

I was glad she liked the latte I had made her.

'I'm thinking a trip north is on the cards soon.'

Eva Black dished up pancakes and bacon, drizzled maple syrup over the top then added a scoop of vanilla ice-cream. Then she brought over two plates to my kitchen table. I followed her with our cups of coffee.

I sat down. As soon as I picked up my knife and fork, the interrogation started.

'You're in Melbourne?'

Yes, I was. But why did it matter?

'I do live here, in this apartment.' Just in case my mother had hit her head recently.

'Why?' My movements never bothered her before; something was going on.

'Why, what?' I needed to find out why my mother needed to know.

'Why are you here?' This meant she knew I had been split-ting my time between Melbourne and Mulwala recently.

'I needed to see Connor.' It was the truth. I also had a few other things to do. So, this trip was as good a time as ever. To sort out what I needed to sort out, like what I was going to do for the rest of my life.

'Oh,' my mother said, then waited for me to continue.

'I'm Connor's business partner. I'm here to sort out the books and get them up to date.'

'Then what are your plans?'

Why was she so concerned about what I was up to? I had never known her to worry about me like this before. But then again, I had never been attacked before.

'Why?' I asked, but Eva Black didn't answer me. She con-tinued with her questions.

'Do you plan on going back?'

Why was it so important that my mother know that?

'Back to Mulwala?'

'Yes.' For the first time in a long time, I saw my mother let out an exasperated breath. It wasn't very often she let her frus-tration show.

'You know I come and go as I need to, the same as Zach.' I had a few things I needed to work out and I wasn't about to give away anything I hadn't worked out first.

'Where's your car, Honeybee? You will need one if you plan to come and go as you please.'

What kind of question was that? Why was the whereabouts of my car so important? What was with my mother and her interrogation? At least it was my mother and not my father. His interrogations were the worst. But I guess my mother had picked up some of his tactics. Argh, there was no hope for me. I just had to figure this out and do it quickly. But maybe that was my mother's whole point to her visit.

'Where it should be.' With Morgan, but I didn't add that.

'It's not downstairs.' My mother pushed carefully.

'I don't need a car.' I threw out to her, a slight irritation in my voice.

'I don't want you in Melbourne without a car.' Why was it so important I had a car? I wanted to ask, but what would be the point. Eva Black wouldn't give up her reason as to why. 'We can go car shopping, then you will have a car.'

'Mum, stop.' I huffed out. Sometimes my mother was exhausting.

'Alex,' my mother used her do-not-test-me voice.

'Morgan has my car, she needed it more than me, you know her brother's an arsehole. I didn't want her to be caught without a car.' Taking a deep breath in and letting it out slowly I continued. 'Brad brought me down. I'll purchase a new car when I'm ready and I promise to be careful until Paul is found. But did you really think that Brad was going to let me out of his sight? I love you and thank you for breakfast.'

What my mother didn't realise was that I planned to spend a lot of time in my apartment and not out and about like she thought. There were a few things I needed to take care of. Then I would make a plan to shop, and at the top of my list would be a car. I wasn't game enough to tell my mother I was about to purchase the latest V8. She didn't understand why I loved that rumble so much.

'I just want you to be safe wherever you are.'

'Okay, Mum. I'll be careful,' came out of my mouth. I even surprised myself with the steady tone of the words I just spoken. My irritation from a moment ago – gone.

Kissing my cheek, my mother left me to clean up our breakfast dishes. Standing at the sink washing up, my mind wandered to last night. I loved that Brad didn't hesitate to take advantage of me being stuck and turn it into something as sexual. I had gotten what I deserved teasing him with my black lingerie, and he teased me right back until he let me come.

The moments Brad and I had shared from the first time to all our Friday night hook-ups, but the morning he surprised me in Mulwala was when our hookups morphed to making love. I knew it was much as I knew Brad knew it. Was I falling or had I already fallen in deep, but was I ready to say the words to him? When was the right time to blurt out those three words for the first time?

My heart had been broken before, and it had taken a long time for it to heal. I didn't think I could take it if it broke again. But what I had to remember was the girl I was then and the woman I was now were two different people. I was stronger now. Mentally and physically. I had built walls, worked on my attitude, and I needed defences for someone to knock down. The right person. The one.

Knowing that I loved Brad and that he was the one for me, I snapped out of my thoughts of him to concentrate on the other things I had to work out.

What I did need to think about was what the hell was I going to do about the ever-growing number of extracurricular activities I now had outside of my fulltime job, which included looking after Connor's money. Zach's businesses were what started my side hustle and ever since I'd been thinking about better ways to handle all of our finances. We were all paid decent wages, Connor, Zach and me, and the amount of debt we each had was minimal.

What would their thoughts be when I told them I wanted to be a qualified financial planner. Could I turn my side hustle into a business? Would it be enough to make a living off? Could I do this, run my own accounting business and expand my recommendations to give financial advice?

The feeling had been there for a while that maybe I had outgrown my love of climbing the corporate ladder with the full-time job I had. Maybe I liked the idea that I could be my own boss. To be able to come and go as I pleased had its own appeal. And knowing my family would benefit from the newly gained skills I would soon have, giving financial advice seemed like the way the forward.

Twenty-three

Lex

Brad watched on as I worked through my Monday morning 'I'm off to the office routine'. I showered, dressed to impress, applied subtle make-up, put my hair in a messy bun and sprayed on perfume. Grabbing my handbag, I made sure I had everything I needed then made my way out of my apartment.

Holding my hand, Brad led me down to his car. He was chauffeuring me around today while I ran errands, and my first stop was Andrews and Co Accounting to see my boss Peyton.

I reached the office where my boss ran her business. My nerves were a little fried by the time I made it inside the building. I counted to ten, then let each breath in and out slowly. My first and only stop was my boss's office, and I wondered if she had any idea of what was about to unfold today.

I knocked and waited for Peyton to look up and signal for me with the flick of her fingers to come into her office. She did and hung up her office phone a moment later.

'Lex.' I could see the surprise on her face. 'It's been a minute. But thank you for your emails and the updates on your accounts.'

'I know I was only meant to have a week away from the office and my absence turned into three weeks. I'm sorry my recent performance has not been of its usual standard.'

Peyton stayed silent. Did she wonder where this conversation would end up? Or did she have no idea?

'I have had to take care of one or two personal matters recently, which is why I'm here.' I stopped for a quick breath and Peyton waited for me to continue. 'I have loved working with you, and I appreciate being able to work from home. But I've decided I need a change of pace. I'm here to give you my two weeks' notice.'

I handed over my letter of resignation.

Peyton looked surprised as I told her my plan to change careers. 'You are my most talented accountant, Lex. I'll be sad to lose you. But I wish you all the best for the future and your next endeavours.'

'I'm going to continue to work from home for the next two weeks. I'll keep my accounts up to date, then I'll bring in what I have at home back to the office. I'll also continue to send emails with the progress I've made.'

'Take care, Lex.' Peyton's goodbye.

'Likewise, Peyton,' I told my boss.

Peyton stood and shook my hand. Then I turned and left her office. A heaviness had been lifted from my shoulders. I was two weeks away from what I was about to do next, and it would come around quicker than expected. I needed to be ready for everything that would be thrown my way.

Brad dropped me off and had waited until I made it through the sliding doors before he drove off. Seeing him pacing the front of Andrews and Co surprised me. I hadn't expected to be chaperoned back to his car, but I liked it and that we were holding hands.

I needed to change out of the business clothes I had chosen to wear today and into something comfortable I could lay on the lounge in. Comfortable was ankle-length leggings, socks to keep my feet from getting cold, a singlet for warmth and a long sleeve tee-shirt, my favourite.

With my coffee in one hand, my notebook and pen in the other and my laptop upon my blanket covered legs, I was ready to go. Firstly, wanted to check the house in Mulwala I had my eye on. Was it still available? It had caught my eye, and I had started to fall in love with it. With my holiday house a revolving door of family coming and going, I wanted something a little quieter where I could run my businesses out of the detached office at the front of the property. I shouldn't have been surprised by what I found, but I was.

The house was under contract. It hadn't even been on the market long. I sighed loudly and let out an exasperated huff.

Bugger.

Did I go on the hunt for another house right this minute? Or did I let it go? I didn't really need a house; I already had one – the one I'd purchased from my parents when they wanted to live in Melbourne full time.

My childhood home held so many memories from growing up to the time Brad and I had spent together. I couldn't let any of those memories go, so my kitchen table would have to suffice until I figured out some sort of office.

I moved on from house hunting as Brad sat down next to me with his laptop in his hand. There was no need for me to get hung up on a house that would never be mine. And I needed to spend these next two weeks establishing my next business adventure. I had already set up Alex Black Accounting from when I'd first started doing Zach's books. But now it was time to kick off my new business and make a name for myself.

Top Shelf Financial Planning.

I wanted to be the woman you came to if you wanted your money sorted. To do that I needed to be more than an accountant, so I wanted to move into personal finance. I was good with my money and the investments I had made from what I had learnt so far with my degree and work experience. I could start with Connor and Zach's money. Manage it for them. Then I could expand and put together financial plans for the rest of my clients if they would let me. If Top Shelf Financial Planning took off, I would have to employ someone to help with my accounting business.

With my two businesses sorted, I created an email address I could use to contact my clients to let them know I was pursuing my own business adventure and that I was going to start charging appropriately for my services. If my family accepted the terms I outlined in my email, I would have a steady stream of income coming in to grow my business to what I wanted it to be.

My next email was to Harley and her mum Mia. I wanted to let them know about my new terms I had put together and give them the option to stay board. I also wanted to let them know about my financial planning services.

With my second latte fixed and my blanket thrown back over my legs, I placed my laptop on my legs, my fingers poised over the keys as I typed a proposal for potential new customers. In my sights was The Grand Hotel. I had already done so much there already, so I just needed the okay to keep up the organisation. But I would save my proposal for when the time was right.

Waking up in bed in my leggings and tee-shirt told me that I had been carried to bed after working on proposals well into the early hours of this morning. I hadn't meant to wear myself out to the point I missed snuggling up to Brad, and now it was mid-morning.

I stretched and wished I could stay here in the comfort of my bed all day. But I had work to do. The quicker I got myself set up with what I needed to do for Top Shelf Financial Planning, the quicker I could pack up, drive out of here, head north and settle into making my house in Mulwala home.

There were a couple of things I had written on my 'to-do list' that I needed to get done today. How long those tasks took to complete would determine the time I stayed in Melbourne.

I got up and worked through my yoga routine before I showered and dressed professionally. I paired my black ballet flats with black underwear, a black pencil skirt, and a blue camisole underneath my matching black jacket. With barely-there make-up and glossy lips, I was ready to go.

Hearing my apartment door open, I found Brad crossing the threshold in sweaty gym clothes.

'Going somewhere?' Brad's gorgeous smile lit up his face.

'I have more errands to run today.'

'You running errands have anything to do with how long you plan on staying in Melbourne?'

'I gave my boss two weeks' notice. So, that's the goal.'

'We'll get what you need done, then you can get ready to move.'

'You're not coming with me?'

'I have case notes for my father to finish first.'

'Okay.' It came out deflated.

'Nothing will keep me from you, Alex. Let me grab a quick shower.'

Brad's words turned my lips upward. I liked the sound of that. He wanted to be together even though my plan wasn't to live in Melbourne anymore. What was Brad up to? Was I entering into a long-distance relationship with this man? Or did he have a plan up his sleeve that he wasn't sharing with me? Maybe he had ducks to line up in a row just like I had to.

I saw the smile that Brad tried to hide the moment we walked into the dealership. I knew exactly what I wanted. Nothing short of top of the line would be acceptable. An SS Holden Commodore sedan. It meant I would have to wait a little under two weeks for delivery. That time frame worked for me even with the modifications I had made. I wanted to squeal in delight. But I didn't. I would do my little victory dance the moment the keys were placed in my hands.

The other two stops on my list today were my mobile phone provider and the bank. I needed an upgrade and a new account. I had to be able to do my job on the move, or out and about. Reception was also high on my priorities as being in a small country town like Mulwala, I needed to be able to reach everyone. Now that I had set up my financial planning business, I had to open a bank account for it.

All that was left to decide was my personalised plates and the design of my business cards. I could do that in the comfort of my own apartment.

On the comfort of my lounge, I debated what personalised plates I wanted for my new black Commodore. Zach had BLK, Connor had his initials CSB. BLACK seemed unoriginal considering the entire car from inside out would be black, and I didn't want to use LEX either. I settled on and ordered A BLK SS.

With Brad beside me working on his case notes, I worked on the design of my business cards until I fell asleep. I picked out everything I wanted to put on both sides, including the words and design. It was late and I wanted fresh eyes to give my handywork one more perusal. I put my laptop aside, and when he reached for my hand, it was time to snuggle up to Brad in bed.

Twenty-four

Brad

'I don't appreciate my daughter being put in unnecessary danger, Mr Waters.' I heard on the other end when I answered my phone. It was no surprise Alex and her siblings lacked the ability of a basic greeting when their father was a master who got straight to the point.

'Alex isn't a caged bird. She will do whatever the bloody hell she wants to, and you know that as well as I do. You raised her to be an independent woman. So, you also know Alex can take care of herself.'

'Paul Christensen is still out there. I want Alex safe.' The words I heard floated through my head, but what ticked over and over was: If you did your job and fucking found Paul, then Alex would be safe.

I wasn't game enough to say that, so instead I responded, 'Your daughter was surrounded by three adult males, and two of those males were her brothers. Did you really think someone would be stupid enough to take us all on? You can't surprise four people and think you will make it out alive, plus the tail you put on Alex makes me doubt Paul would have gotten too close.' I ran hand over my face, whiskers prickling the palm of my hand. I still hadn't shaved my face.

'I wouldn't put anything past the prick who hurt Alex and Connor. Her little reunion with Connor piqued Paul's interest,' Detective Black's unimpressed voice told me, before he continued. 'My concern is that because Alex chose you to cosy up to and now that you two have grown close, Paul isn't a big fan of yours either.'

'Good, maybe you can use that to your advantage.' If Paul had me in his sights, I needed to be careful. If I was caught in Paul's crosshairs, a surprise attack may be in my future. I better not let him find out she enjoyed me, my body and my fingers as I explored all of her curves and made her come, more than once. Paul might go ballistic. Fuck him, anyway, for thinking he'd ever had a chance with Alex. Dumb fuck should never have laid a finger on her or let thoughts of Alex cross his mind.

'You had us followed last night?' My words made me sound more surprised than I felt. I knew Detective Black would stop at nothing to get what he wanted.

'The tail was on Connor, that's how I knew Alex was back in Melbourne and standing outside The Groove with you and Zach. Paul showed up but slipped out of sight of the plain clothes police when you all got into Zach's truck.'

When Zach offered everyone a ride home, I was grateful. Without Zach, I was the only one sober. There was no way I would have been able to keep both Connor and Alex safe if we had of walked home.

'You called, I answered. Was there a reason? Or did you just want to lecture me?' When I opened my mouth the words just fell out. I didn't want to go toe to toe with Alex's dad. That was not my plan. As much as I wanted to give Detective Black a piece of my mind, I knew if I held my tongue, it would save my skin – if I ever saw him again.

'I want to catch a criminal, Mr Waters.' The detective threw his frustration my way. It seemed he was no closer to catching Paul.

'What do you suggest then?' But I doubted that Preston Black was about to elaborate. It was useless; the man gave nothing away. He was silent. I listened for a few moments and when Detective Black didn't say anything, I continued, because I couldn't help myself. 'Unless Paul doesn't really want to hurt Alex, because he still has unfinished business with Connor: the money. Makes sense if Paul thinks he's been hard done by. If he believes Connor really cares about how much money he has in the bank, then what better way to get back at Connor than to go after his money. Alex would only be useful if Paul thought she had access to Connor's money – and maybe not just Connor's money. Alex is an accountant. She does have access to most of her family's money.'

I voiced my thoughts as they came to mind. When I finished, I closed my mouth. Silence fell over both of us. No one spoke, and all I could hear was the detective as he paced. Was he still deep in thought?

I continued, 'I'm already staying with Alex, and Paul has seen us together. Maybe he's just stupid enough to try a surprise attack on me.' I waited to see if Detective Black was listening.

When I heard no response from him, I took a chance and hung up. If he thought over what I'd said, then he would put a tail on me.

I knew Alex's plan. She was waiting on a call to say her car was ready and then she was leaving for Mulwala. I would spend the next couple of weeks with Alex, waking up in bed with her, starting our days together, working alongside her on the lounge– when in reality I didn't have a job. What I was working on was my case files for my father. Finishing my day with Alex in my arms was what I wanted for the rest of my life.

I threw my phone on the bed in my apartment and paced as I thought about Alex. I had left her as she had been working away at her kitchen table when I decided I needed more clothes. That arsehole better not hurt her again. My thoughts were interrupted by a knock on my apartment door. My heart rate spiked as I looked through the peep hole. I took a deep breath, and the beat of my heart slowed slightly, then I opened the door to my mother who stood in the doorway, unimpressed.

Maggie Waters kissed my check as she walked past. I closed the door and followed her to the lounge where she had sat down.

'I know you and your father don't always see eye to eye, but did you really have to quit?'

There was no point skirting around the truth. I had no reason to lie to her. I sat down on the lounge beside her and answered, 'Yes.'

'You love your job. What changed?' My mother needed me to explain to her why I was about the throw away a career that she had paved out with the help of my father.

'I don't want to spend the rest of my life at work,' I started, but was interrupted.

'You met someone?' I don't know how Maggie Waters knew, but she did. Maybe it was the look on my face as thoughts of Alex came to mind and stuck in my head.

'I met a woman, and she is more important to me than the hours Dad makes me spend at the office.'

'You need to tell your father.'

'No.' My answer was harsh, but I wanted out of the family business. I wanted to stand on my own two feet. I would always be a lawyer, but now I could be a lawyer on my own terms.

'Is she the one? Do you love her?' My mother was curious about the woman I had met and hadn't told her about.

I didn't want to admit to her first that Alex was the woman for me. All I wanted to do was tell Alex how I felt about her. But I couldn't ignore her, not when she sat near me. 'She is, and I do.' And before my mother could interrupt me again, I said, 'And the funny thing is, I haven't even told her I love her yet.'

Maggie Waters reached over and squeezed my hand. Was that a sign of her approval? She never showed affection. My father had made my mother a complicated woman with hardened edges. But I always knew she loved me, in her own way.

William Waters was a hard man. It was what had been passed down generation after generation. My mother loved him anyway, and my father made sure we never went without except for that he was always at work.

'Your father will not be happy I'm here, nor will he be impressed when he finds out I have told you this.' My mother never defied my father; they were always on the same team.

I was curious what Maggie Waters knew that I didn't, but I wasn't prepared to ask her.

'Your father and I had always hoped that you would follow in his footsteps. However, in case you wanted to travel, or you wanted a different career, I made your father set up an account for you to use if you ever chose another path. But you had to prove to either of us that you wouldn't waste the money.'

I wanted to open my mouth and say something to her, but no words came out. She, on the other hand, hadn't finished speaking.

'I came here to try and convince you not to throw away the job you love so much. But as I look around me, I can see that you haven't made this apartment your own. That tells me you are not as happy as you should be, and that's usually because there is something missing in your life.'

My mother reached into her handbag and pulled out a piece of paper. She placed the paper on the lounge between us. Did I dare to look at it right now or did I save it for after she left?

Maggie Waters stood and so did I. Before she had a chance to move, I reached out and hugged her. 'I promise not to let you down,' I said as I pulled back from her.

'I know you won't.' She kissed my cheek once more before she made her way out of my apartment.

At the sound of my front door as it closed, I leaned down to pick up the piece of paper. Unfolding it, I read what was in front of me. Details of an account jumped out from the page. It was money I could use as a deposit, and with the money I had saved and hadn't spent on this apartment, I could fill my house with every piece of furniture I could ever dream of. Any money left over I could put towards a new career. I was spoilt for choice. Now all I had to do was put everything in place.

Twenty-five

Lex

My last day of work came around quicker than I thought it would. But I was glad all my accounts were up to date. I had plenty to do once I had decided to focus on Black Label Accounting as my sole source of income and relocate myself north. I knew I had my work cut out for me.

My 'to-do list' grew longer, so I had plenty of tasks to keep me going. I had both my business ventures to work on and my apartment to clean up and leave neat and tidy. I packed up a few things from my apartment, mainly my small office and most of my clothes, then loaded up the boot of my brand-new car with what I thought I needed to take with me. The rest I would sort out with the trips I knew I would make back and forth.

My plan, on my way out of town, was to drop off the things I had collected from my years of work I had done for Peyton, her laptop included. With quick goodbyes to everyone I had worked with over the years, I was on the road heading north to the change in pace I wanted from my lifestyle.

The only thing missing was Brad. He had spent every night for the last two weeks with me. We were getting to know each other better and more intimately. My arms were either around him or his arms were around me. We were getting a feel for what it would be like living with each other every day. I wanted that, I wanted Brad to tease me until I came or push my sleep shorts aside to enter me from behind, and I wanted to wake Brad with my lips around his cock. But I knew I was leaving, and Brad had to stay for work. One day I told myself everything would be perfect. My businesses would be successful, and Brad would be here with me by my side.

I tried not to dwell on what I was leaving behind; instead, I texted Morgan and Harley to tell them both that we were over-due for a catch up. We needed to celebrate the next exciting phase of my life. With Morgan's help, I requested a few groceries. My plan was to make a breakfast feast, then chill out and maybe play my guitar and hope my sisters-to-be would be good sports and join me, or stick around while I blew off some my lonely frustrations.

There was just one stop I had to make on my way to my childhood house in Mulwala by the river, and that was to see Jaime. I wanted to know how he was going since I had been there last when Morgan's brother smashed her phone, and glass had cut up the area near her eye.

I made good time tonight even though I felt everyone want-ed to go the same way that I was going. There wasn't a need to rush, and I would get there when I got there. When I saw my brother's business in the distance, Black's Bar and Grill, I knew it wouldn't be long before I crossed the bridge. I was on the home stretch now.

I parked my car behind The Grand. My home screen lit up and that's when I saw I had an unread message.

My brother.

Z: Harley tells me you're in town. Will you play at my event tomorrow?

L: Zach, I would love to but I haven't played in ages. It would be messy.

Z: I know you have practice lined up for tomorrow and I know you always support my events. So please Lexie will you play?

L: I don't really have a choice, do I?

Z: Not really.

L: Okay, I guess I will see you tomorrow.

Z: Thanks Lex. See you tomorrow.

Before I threw my phone back into my handbag, I texted Brad.

L: I'm here.

B: You made good timing.

L: The car did well.

B: Only you would drive the car straight off the lot and north.

L: I need to know the car will handle anything.

B: Be safe, Alex.

L: Always.

Getting out of my car, I locked the doors with my key fob and walked around to The Grand's main entrance. I found

Jaime behind the bar, the same as the last time I was here with Morgan. I waved my hello.

Jaime offered his hello as he saw me approach the bar.

'You look hungry? Are you hungry?'

'What are you up to, Jaime?' I asked as I watched him disappear from behind the bar and come out the employee-only area near the bistro.

'I'm about to close, and I have leftovers from tonight's dinner rush. Please let me whip you up something. You can even take it home to eat if you like.'

'Sure,' I agreed, and Jaime took my hand and led me into the pub's kitchen.

'Stay right here.' He entered the kitchen and left me standing just inside the door as he went to make dinner. 'I want to talk, and I want to surprise you,' Jaime explained, so I wasn't getting the cold shoulder.

'What's going on with you?' I was curious to know what had gotten into Jaime. I tried to look at what he was up to, but it was useless as I couldn't see anything from where I stood.

'I talked to my mum,' Jaime started to say, and it was anyone's guess where this would end up. 'I've been to see her too.' I watched as Jaime moved around the kitchen. He had come to know me so well. 'I told her about the front bar and that Connor had bailed us out, even though she fired him.'

Jaime disappeared from sight, moved to get something from the fridge before he came back to the prep area he was using. His eyes found mine before he continued to speak. 'I was a little worried Mum would lose her shit when I told her.'

Here we go, I thought while Jaime spoke.

'I have single-handedly run the bistro for the last three weeks.'

'The suspense is killing me, Jaime.' I said over the noise of food sizzling on the hotplate.

'At first Mum wasn't happy. But when I explained it was only for dinner and that the bar wasn't open unless you purchased a meal, she seemed to calm down.' Jaime threw his biggest smile my way, before he continued. 'That was when I decided to go for it and ask Mum for a job in the kitchen.'

'And what did she say?' I was alternating on chewing my fingernails and bottom lip.

'That she would like to see me run the bistro single-handedly.' Jaime's smile slipped from his face. 'She will be back tomorrow with Jarryd and Jason. Jason got his learners while he was in Melbourne and Mum's going to let him drive her home. So, they'll be here to watch me manage the dinner rush.'

Jaime had finished whatever he had concocted and signalled me to come closer with the come-here gesture of his fingers. 'Jaime, you should be proud.' I stepped forward. He had made two steak sandwiches. One for me and one for himself.

With a plate in each hand, I followed Jaime into the dining room and sat down at a table close to the kitchen. Jaime, however, put down our food and then disappeared. A few minutes later he reappeared with a beer in one hand and a glass of wine in the other.

'To new beginnings.' Jaime toasted, still smiling like an idiot.

'To new beginnings,' I copied, my small smile nothing like Jaime's.

'I may have also mentioned to Mum that you have been helping out with the office,' Jaime said before he picked up his sandwich and took a bite.

I sighed before I took a bite of mine. The family trademark one eyebrow was raised as I looked at him.

'I'm sorry, I know you wanted to talk to my mum when you were ready, but she was curious to know how Connor had bailed us out. That's when I told Mum that you had worked your accountancy and financial magic. Well, now Mum wants to see what you've done to her office.'

I didn't know what to say, so I sipped on my wine.

'I guess my mum will see what I mean when she gets home tomorrow.'

'Well, I hope she doesn't freak out too much. I still have files at my place that I need to bring back.'

'Bring them back tomorrow, then you can meet her and talk to her,' Jaime said as he took both of our plates into the kitchen.

'I think we both know that's not a good idea,' I told Jaime when he came back from the kitchen.

'Okay.' His response was deflated. His forehead creased as he thought things over.

I finished my wine, my pointed finger pressed into Jaime's his chest. There was something I needed to explain to him. 'Tomorrow is going to be a long day for your mum. She'll be tired and she'll probably want some quiet time with her family.'

'Are you saying I shouldn't open for dinner?' Jaime's eyebrows knitted.

'You want to impress your mother. Surprise her, show off your talent as chef. Just don't scare her. She doesn't need another heart attack. Okay.'

Jaime was quiet. I stood up, ready to leave. As I walked past Jaime, he called my name. He hugged me goodbye and when he let me go, he said, 'Thanks, you've given me an idea.'

'You're welcome, thanks for dinner.' I offered another small smile as exhaustion started to creep in. I was glad my house wasn't too far away.

I pulled into my drive, waited for my garage door to open and parked my new car next to the other car in my garage – my black Commodore wagon I had left for Morgan to drive. Morgan was here. It would be good to see her, see how she was holding up without my brother.

Morgan was on the lounge when I walked in from the garage. There was small amount of disappointment on her face when she saw it was me and not Connor. But it didn't stop her from jumping up to hug me hello. 'Have you eaten? I have leftovers.'

'I've eaten.'

Morgan released me and went to the fridge to pour two glasses of wine. 'Here, you look like you need this,' I was told as the wine glass was placed in my hand.

'I'm going to take this, run a bath and unwind before I call it a night,' I said as I sipped on more wine.

'You want to take the rest of bottle with you?' Morgan asked like she knew the bottle would offer the comfort I needed. But I knew better.

'Zach wants me to play at his event tomorrow, and I'm a little rusty. Maybe I should just stick to one glass,' I said as made my way to the master bedroom. My room.

Twenty-six

Lex

To say I was ready by the time Harley had arrived was laughable. I had woken only a few minutes prior. At least I was out of bed, with my dressing gown wrapped around me. I had fallen asleep thinking about Brad and how he would distract me while sitting on the lounge next to me. He had done it several times in the last two weeks. He would close my laptop pull my legs until I was laying down on the lounge, then he would make love to me.

For the first time in a long time, I had slept a solid twelve hours. I woke refreshed, but now I was in a rush to catch up. I was meant to be up early before everyone got here to make a start on breakfast.

I would have to impress another day with my early-bird organisation. Today I just needed to get out there and make a start to the day. I moved out of my bedroom to say hello to Harley. She hugged me, with an added squeeze before she let me go.

'Hope you don't mind,' Harley said as we separated. 'I brought someone who needed some cheering up.' Harley moved aside for me to see a woman who stood just inside my front door.

'Of course not, the more the merrier,' I said as I saw Morgan come down the stairs at the sound of Harley and me talking.

'Lex, you remember Shea?'

'It's been a while since I've been here,' Shea admitted.

'You and Zach did Year 12 together. I've seen you around at a few of Zach's events.'

'I can't let the boys have all the fun.' Shea smirked her cheekiness.

When Morgan reached the bottom stair, she took the silence as an opportunity to introduce herself. 'I'm Morgan.'

'Morgan is Connor's woman,' I offered to Harley, as a way to explain Morgan's presence.

'I'm Harley, Zach's woman,' she said as she stepped closer to Morgan.

Morgan didn't argue that she wasn't Connor's woman, just stuck her hand out for Harley to shake. 'Woman, I'm not shaking your hand. Come give me hug.'

Morgan didn't argue with Harley either, just stepped forward and hugged Harley.

'Morgan, this is Shea. Shea, this is Morgan.' Harley made the introductions as both women waved their hellos at each other.

When the introductions had been made, I stepped closer to Shea. She had tears in her eyes. I hugged her. I couldn't help but offer some sort of comfort, same as I had done with Morgan.

Shea wiped her eyes when I let her go and whispered, 'Thank you.'

'Shea's a family friend, and she owns the dress shop in the main street,' Harley told Morgan.

'I'm a primary school teacher, and I think Connor bought my clothes from your shop.' Morgan pointed to the clothes she was wearing. Shea nodded her confirmation.

'Yeah, Connor instructed me to put some clothes together and send them over. I've just been waiting for our new season stock to arrive before I put something together for you,' Shea told Morgan.

'I would love to come in to see what you've got,' Morgan replied.

'Let me know when you're free and we can do a one-on-one session after hours if that works.' Morgan nodded that she was interested. 'Actually, if any of you ladies are interested in an after-hours one-on-one style session let me know.

'That sounds awesome,' I told Shea.

'Lex, will you please go and get dressed,' Harley said as she turned to face me. 'I'll make coffees for everyone. Hurry up. Go.'

I smiled at Harley's bossiness. She wasn't the shy woman I once knew. My brother had rubbed off on her. She was happy, and I was happy for her.

I showered and dressed in comfortable underwear, found ankle-length leggings and a singlet to wear. I slipped my kimono over my shoulders and wrapped it around me. Later I would pull off my kimono and slip into my favourite off-the-shoulder jumper that was long enough to cover my bottom. But for now, I was comfortable in my black attire and bright purple kimono.

I coated my lashes in mascara and filled in my eyebrows. I applied highlighter to my cheekbones and reached for my nude-coloured lip gloss. I knew I was about to eat but I wanted to look like I was ready to take on the world even if I didn't feel like I was ready.

The coffee Harley had made filled my kitchen and made my house smell amazing. I couldn't help but smile as Harley approached with a coffee cup in her hand.

'Latte with a touch of chocolate and hazelnut.'

'Thank you,' I said and took a sip.

The hot liquid was the kickstart I needed to get my head over my insecurities to where I needed it to be: the here and now. I downed the rest of my coffee and got to work on the feast, I'd told Harley and Morgan, I would make them.

Harley, Morgan and Shea sat around my island bench and chatted as I fell into a rhythm and moved around my kitchen with ease. I made pancakes, French toast, scrambled eggs, bacon, toast, hash browns and sausages.

The conversation continued as we ate breakfast outside.

'Thanks for breakfast,' these beautiful women said in unison, once I had sat down with them to eat.

'You ladies are most welcome,' I told them before I dropped my bombshell. 'Now that breakfast is almost out of the way, you can all help me sort out a playlist for today's event.'

'I knew there was a reason you wanted to hang with us,' Harley said before a laugh escaped her.

'Event?' Morgan asked horrified, the small shake of her body didn't escape me.

'Morgan.' I reached out my fingers to touch her forearm to reassure her. She didn't know the inner workings of my family though she would get used to them the longer she dated my brother. 'My brother Zach puts on music events from time to time, roughly every three months, at his business Black's Bar and Grill. Harley and I are playing today.'

'I'm playing too,' Shea added.

'Harley, Shea and I are going to kick back before the event and play our guitars. You are welcome to join us.'

'I can hang out and play my guitar with you, but the event,' Morgan's voice had trailed off. 'Please don't make me go,' she whispered.

I moved my hand to cover Morgan's and squeezed until she looked up at me. 'Honey, no one is making you do anything you don't want to do. Except for our jam session; you don't have a choice in that.'

Morgan wiped her tears away and tipped her lips into a small smile. There was no way I would force her to do anything. Plus, she might have already made plans for this afternoon.

Packing up our plates we took them back inside. There wasn't much food left, and I was glad I didn't have to pack too much up. While Morgan stacked the dishwasher, I packed the leftovers into the fridge and Harley made more coffees.

When my kitchen was clean, everyone went to get their guitars. Mine was packed away in my room. Harley's and Shea's must have been in Harley's car in preparation for the event. Morgan raced upstairs to her bedroom to get my old guitar. The guitar in my room was new; I hadn't broken it in yet. Apart from the few lessons I had given Morgan, I hadn't played it much. My new acoustic guitar was matte black with my initials engraved just below the strings.

We dragged lounge chairs from my patio into my large backyard and sat in circle so we could see each other. When we were all comfortable, I started to strum my guitar. It had been a while, and my guitar needed a slight tune. When the others had done the same, I got this show on the road.

'You girls got your songs picked out for Zach's event?' I asked Shea and Harley.

Both women nodded, but they didn't let on what songs they'd picked. I would have to wait for the event to hear their choice of covers.

'Well, now you can help me.' I smirked at them. Stuff them. Their silence would only spur me on. Something I needed to get me through the rest of today.

'What about the song I gave you?' Harley asked me.

'Maddie and Tae's "Bathroom Floor"?' I asked, looking at Morgan. Was she ready to show me how much she had learnt?

I turned to face Harley, nodded, then strummed the first few cords on my guitar.

When I turned back to Morgan, I could see her fingers on her guitar; she had decided to join me and play. I belted out the lyrics and Morgan sang with me. Her voice was beautiful as my backup. Though if she ever wanted to get up and sing at one of Zach's events then I would stand beside her and be her backup. Especially if she wanted to play Sarah McLachlan's 'Angel'.

'That was you at the hospital?' Harley asked as Morgan blushed. 'Your voice is angelic.'

'Thank you.' Morgan offered a sweet smile to Harley.

'As for you Lex,' Harley said, 'there's no doubt you're confident with the guitar. Today should be no pressure for you.'

Harley's smirk was wicked before she stuck out her tongue at me.

'Have you got any idea what you want to play today?' Shea asked.

Without a reply I let my fingers dance along my guitar. I was glad when the girls joined me in singing and playing their guitars to 'Yeah Boy' by Kelsey Ballerini.

'I don't think you really needed our help.' Morgan eyed me.

'I needed to jam, that much is true, as for which songs I'm going to play, I don't know. I haven't learnt anything new in ages. I might have to pull out some old favourites.'

'With your talent I'm sure you won't disappoint today.' Shea's words were a boost to my confidence. 'Good luck out there.'

'You too, knock 'em dead,' I told Shea as we all packed up our guitars.

'Shea and I best get going,' Harley told Morgan and me.

'No worries, I'll meet you there.' I followed them out to Harley's car in my driveway and waved goodbye.

'Will you be okay?' I couldn't help but ask Morgan. I was about to leave Morgan on her own while I attended my brother's event at Black's Bar and Grill.

'I have my classes to plan and tests to mark, so the peace and quiet will help,' Morgan said from where she stood in my kitchen.

'Well, feel free to spread yourself out all over my kitchen table. I think I have packed everything up.'

'Thanks, I will do.'

'Hey, good job out there today. I could tell you've been practising. You will be a pro in no time.' A cheeky grin spread on my face.

'I'm learning a new song,' Morgan told me.

'Teaching yourself?' I asked.

'I want to play Sarah McLachlan's "Angel" for Connor,' Morgan told me. 'One day, when I'm ready.'

'That's awesome.' I secretly wished I could sing that song with her.

'Thank you for today. It was a lot of fun hanging out, and practising has been a great stress relief.'

'It's how I got through uni.'

'Then go and show them all your amazing talent,' Morgan said as she tried to hurry me out the garage door.

But first I had to unpack the boot of my car and dump everything into my bedroom. Then change into my off-the-shoulder jumper. Now it was time to go. I put my guitar in the boot and my handbag on the seat next to me. Time to get this event over with. How hard could it be for me to play three songs?

I pulled out of my driveway and made my way to Black's Bar and Grill. The carpark of Zach's business had filled up quickly for his event. I made my way down to the bottom level of the carpark to find what I needed. An empty spot. I grabbed my handbag, then my guitar, and I headed up the stairs to the front doors.

I made my way to The Graphite Beer Garden. The crowd had already started to build, and my brother looked like he was ready to get this show on the road. I headed to the bar to order myself a glass of wine, something to help knock off the edge of how I felt now that I was here.

'Show time,' Harley said as she came up to stand beside me at the bar. She took my guitar and put it beside the stage with the other guitars.

We watched as Zach played his three songs. Harley was completely mesmerised by Zach. The two of them were hopelessly in love and completely happy.

'You're on after me,' Harley nudged me with an elbow to my ribs.

Raising my eyebrow to let Harley know I was unimpressed, she turned and walked away from me. No doubt off to find Zach before she got up to sing. *Great.* There was no getting out of this event now.

I watched as Brock, Shea and Harley all played their sets. Zach had surprised Harley on stage. Those two looked so good together and not just as a couple but on stage as a duet. Their chemistry was off the charts. And their voices together were amazing.

Harley and Zach left the stage, and that was my cue.

It was time.

My time to get up there and sing my three songs. I made my way to my guitar, pulled it out of its case and walked up the stairs of the stage when the emcee called my name.

'For those who don't know me, I'm Lex Black,' I said into the microphone, and the crowd clapped and cheered. 'I've been invited to play for you today. I hope you like the songs I've chosen. They are a couple of old favourites of mine.'

And without further ado, I pulled the stool closer to the microphone, put my guitar on my knee and pulled the microphone closer to my mouth. I strummed out the first couple of cords to the first song I'd decided to play.

My set list was:

1. 'Cowboy Take Me Away' – The Chicks
2. 'I Ain't Ready to Quit' – Jason Aldean
3. 'Somebody Like You' – Keith Urban

I paused at the end of 'Somebody like you' and wondered if I should play the end verse. When I heard, 'Don't forget about the bit at the end,' I knew it was Zach heckling me. I knew he would try to stick it to me since I had ambushed one of his last events with Connor. So, without hesitation, I continued on with the last bit of the song I was playing. I was just glad I could hear Zach singing along with me.

I thanked the crowd and left the stage. When I returned from putting my guitar in my car, I found Shea at the bar, a glass already in her hand. I joined her and ordered my own drink. I was just stupid enough to get a little more than tipsy.

'Are we celebrating or commiserating?' I asked as the bartender placed my Jim Beam Black on ice on top of the bar.

Shea gave me her side eye but didn't speak.

'I can go if you want to be alone.' I reached out to grab my drink, about to walk away.

'Here's to love staring me straight in the face and not even knowing it.'

I turned back to look at Shea. 'Guess that means you're not celebrating? Well, if it helps, you're not the only one in that dilemma.'

'What are you going to do about it?' Shea asked like maybe my advice might help her.

'Tell him how I feel the next time I see him,' I explained, then took a sip of my bourbon. 'Even if I don't know when that will be. But I think what I feel might just be the beginning.'

'You sound in love. Like you have it all figured out.' Shea looked at me in despair. Was that a tear I saw in her eye?

'What have you got left to figure out?' I asked, and wondered what was so hard.

'A way to tell him how I feel.' Shea sniffled then sipped on her amber liquid.

'What's so hard about that?' I couldn't help but ask.

'Apart from today, I haven't seen him in a while, and you know how small this town is.' Shea had downed the last of her drink and signalled to the bartender she wanted another one.

'Maybe he's just been busy.' I tried to offer a possible answer. A truth to my own situation. One I had not thought about before.

'Or avoiding me would be more like it.' It was clear Shea was frustrated. It was no wonder she was drinking.

'What makes you think that?' *Why would anyone avoid her?* She was a beautiful and talented woman.

'Because I thought I was just another one-night stand to him.' Shea winced at the words she had heard herself say. 'So stupid,' she said to herself.

'And,' I pried. I could see there was more to this story than Shea was letting on.

'He thinks I'm hung up over Zach.' Shea covered her face with her hands and shook her head.

'Are you?' I was curious to know the answer to this. A lot of women over the years have had their eyes on my brother. But he'd never chased any of them.

'Maybe once a upon a time.' Shea let out a huff. 'But anyone who is a friend of Zach's knows he is hung up on only one woman.'

'Harley,' I said.

Shea nodded.

'Now I don't know what to do,' Shea confessed.

So, I offered a solution. 'If you like this man of yours, then go up to him, grab his shirt and pull him in close and kiss him.'

My bourbons on ice had loosened my tongue. I thought I was funny; Shea though, not so much.

'Must not be so funny if only one person is laughing,' the male voice said when he was close enough to Shea and me. Out the corner of my blurry eye I saw one of Zach's friends had approached.

Shea recognised his voice and smirked my way before she swung herself around on her stool and said, 'Please take me home. I think I may have had enough now.'

'Alcohol or conversation?' he asked as if Shea was drunk, and I was bothering her.

'Does it matter?' Shea replied, and I would have to be blind if I didn't see this was the lifeline that Shea needed.

'Just kiss him already, will you,' I said to Shea, and quickly covered my mouth with my hand. That fell out and now I wondered if I needed to take it back.

There was silence behind me. I hadn't swung myself around like Shea had done. Did I dare turn round? What would I see? When I turned my head, I saw nothing. Shea and my brother's friend had gone. I threw my head back, looked up and wished her good luck.

Now that our conversation was over, and I was all alone, there was only one thing I wished for: to be stolen away, the same way as Shea. But when no one came to rescue me, I ordered another black label bourbon on ice. When my drink did nothing to drown my sorrow, I stepped off the stool I sat on and took myself home.

Twenty-seven

Brad

'You want to tell me why the hell I'm here, Brad?' I shouldn't be shocked by the words that came out of Alex's mouth, but I was.

I had never heard Alex speak that way. Something was wrong. She wasn't her normal bubbly self. Was she hung over from her brother's event last night? Or just annoyed at being interrupted?

'I can explain,' I told Alex. She had no idea why I had changed her plans for today and dragged her away from the business ventures she was very busy trying to build. One of which Alex had told me very little about.

'Please do.' Alex's pointed her sunglass-covered face at me and gave me her attitude.

'We are here to look at the house.' My answer to Alex was vague. I didn't want to give too much of my surprise away, but my vagueness only made Alex crankier.

'This house has been sold, Brad.' Alex's hand landed on her hip the same time as she raised her trademark eyebrow. Alex even pulled her sunglasses down to emphasise she wasn't impressed. Then on a frustrated breath, Alex said, 'I don't have time for this.'

I moved closer to her. As sexy as she was frustrated, I was afraid she would walk away before I had the chance to show her what I wanted to show her. I cupped her neck and ran my thumbs along her jaw before I threaded my fingers into her hair. Tightening the grip, I had on her, I needed her closer for my next words to sink in, but I also wanted her to lose her attitude with me. My plan was only to help. But maybe I had taken my plans a little too far.

'The house has been sold because I bought it.' I whispered my words in the shell of Alex's ear, then I waited for her to respond.

'What! Why?' I was close enough to see the change on her face. But she was damned if she would let me see the emotions in her eyes before they rolled over her face. She pushed her sunglasses higher up her nose to hide her eyes.

'I wanted to surprise you.' Every word I spoke was the opposite of Alex's. I needed to be the calm in the middle of the storm that raged around her. I needed to be her anchor that held her in place when her whirlwind stopped spinning.

'Well, I'm surprised.' Alex's words came out narky, but I guess to her I deserved what she threw at me.

'Alex,' I clipped her name, and her eyes slowly came to look up at mine.

'That's my dream house. Did you know that?' Alex stated as she pointed her hand over my shoulder to the house behind me.

The truth. Alex needed me to tell her the truth. 'Yes,' I softly said before she could push me off her and walk away. 'One of the nights I picked you up from your kitchen table and put you to bed, you had left your computer open and that's when I saw this house. I must admit though – one glance and I was interested. I memorised the details and organised to come and have a look. I knew then that I just had to have it.'

'Congratulations,' Alex told me, but nothing about this moment gave us a reason to celebrate. I needed to find a way for Alex and me to be on the same page. The longer Alex was away from her makeshift kitchen table home office the more I felt her mood would decline.

'Alex,' her name came out just above a whisper. But her eyes didn't lock on to mine like a moment ago. I pushed her sunglasses to the top of her head and used my thumb to push her jaw up.

Alex tried to pull away and argue with me. But I didn't give her a chance to respond. I just brought my other hand up to her face and pulled her lips towards mine. I just hoped Alex would let me kiss her and not fight me on this too.

My lips moved over hers and I waited for the moment it took for Alex to realise I had stopped talking. The moment I felt Alex's hands grip the lapels of my suit, I brushed my tongue over her bottom lip. Then I waited for her tongue to meet mine. Waited for the zap of electricity I would receive when her tongue reached mine.

Our tongues danced as our lips moved in the hungriest way. I closed my teeth over Alex's bottom lip, and I waited for her to pull back. I waited for her 'ouch'. But it didn't come.

'I don't want to stand here and fight all afternoon. I just want you to take me home.' Alex's words didn't surprise me. I knew she had plenty of work to do. But I didn't hesitate to reach out and pick this woman up. Alex's legs automatically wrapped around me.

I didn't take her towards the house and show her around like I know I should have. No, I took her somewhere closer. The office. Our office. Alex just didn't know that yet. She didn't know I was about to become her employee. I just had to pitch my idea to her, but I hoped with the money she didn't have to borrow for this house, she could use towards the businesses she was trying build. Including the one she had started in the two weeks we'd lived in her apartment together. There would be time to talk about that and time to convince Alex to hire me. Right after I made love to this beautiful woman.

Walking us up the steps of the office veranda, I opened the door, and as soon as I was over the threshold, I closed and locked the door. Today wouldn't be the day we got caught. I moved closer to the only furniture in here, the desk, the one that was left behind that would possibly be my desk if Alex said yes.

Laying Alex down, I pushed her until her back was flat against the desk. Her sunglasses fell from her head and landed somewhere behind her. I pulled her long silky legs until they hung over the edge and Alex's butt was just where I wanted it. Then pushed the edge of the skirt Alex chose to wear today until I saw the black lacy G-string she'd also chosen. It was the same scrap of lace I had ripped off her weeks earlier.

Kneeling down, I needed to taste her. I pushed her G-string aside, and the fingers on both of my hands exposed Alex's most delicate area to me. I flicked my tongue out and licked upwards from the entrance of her sex to the nub of her clit and back again.

I was going to push her to the edge and then pull her back. I would tease her for the attitude she used on me, and only when I heard her say my name, I would let her come.

'Oh my,' fell from Alex's mouth. She enjoyed my tongue on her. Time to mix it up a bit. I pulled hard on her G-string, and it broke. Alex didn't complain. Besides, I would buy more, just to tear them off her. I moved my hands up over her hips and dug my fingers into her skin, lavishing Alex's sex. I wanted to feel her come on my tongue.

'Oh, oh,' Alex said breathlessly, and I felt that she might be close. The sound that fell from her mouth did something to me. I was hard from the moment I picked Alex up, and now it was painful. I had to find a way to be inside of her and soon.

'Let it go, Alex,' I grunted out between gritted teeth because I knew if she panted again, I would lose it.

'Brad.' My name was a whisper out of my woman's mouth.

'I know you want to. Let me feel you come.' On command, I felt Alex let go. Felt her muscles spasm under me. I pushed her further but kept the movement of my tongue steady. I wanted to feel her body shake, then I knew I had satisfied her.

'Ahh,' was the sweetest sound I had ever heard, and it had just come out of Alex's mouth. Her body still shook on the other side of her release. Now I wanted more.

'I want you.' I licked my lips as I stood up. This woman tasted so good. Would I ever be able to get enough of her? 'I want you more than I have ever wanted anyone.'

My words made Alex sit up. Her eyes ran over me, from my eyes to my feet and back again, and it was me this time who shivered. Alex grabbed the lapels of my suit jacket as her lips reached for my ear.

'What's with the suit?'

'There's only one reason I wear a suit, baby cakes.' I told Alex. 'And that's for work.' Today was the day I handed over the keys to the apartment and packed up my office and handed in my case notes. Hence the reason I was wearing in a suit.

I watched as Alex moved off the desk to come and stand in front of me. She pushed my suit jacket back over my shoulders and down my arms. My jacket hit the floor a moment later. Alex's hands landed on my belt buckle.

'Alex?' I looked down to see her hands had stilled.

'Shh.' It was a whisper. 'You've had your fun, now it's my turn.' I didn't miss the sexy smile on her face as she turned it away from me.

I should have known that Alex wouldn't undo my belt; she just wanted to untuck me. Pull my white shirt out from my black pants. Before she could undo the buttons of my shirt, she had to loosen my tie. With the knot gone, it fell to the floor.

Alex took her time to undo my shirt buttons, and just like my suit jacket, she pushed my shirt back over my shoulders and down my arms and let the material fall to the ground. It landed on top of my jacket and tie.

Her hands landed on my chest, but she didn't touch naked skin. There was one more piece of material. My Bonds tee-shirt. I knew Alex had more than enjoyed stripping me, but I couldn't help to reach behind me and pull my tee-shirt over my head.

'Stop,' Alex quietly demanded of me, and I couldn't help but raise my eyebrow at her. 'You're going to ruin my fantasy.'

Fantasy. Huh. My cock pulsed. If Alex wanted to strip me, she could finish as soon as I kissed her. I pushed Alex back against the edge of the desk.

But she stood her ground this time and wouldn't let me push her back against the top of the desk. With my right hand, I cupped her face and brought her lips to meet mine. I kissed her until she was breathless, then I let her go. This was a fantasy for Alex, and she wouldn't want it to end too soon. I had to remember that she was calling the shots and not take over.

'That was hot,' Alex whispered, her fingers now running down my naked chest to my belt buckle where this time she did undo it.

Alex didn't bother to pull the belt out from my pants. She dived into the button and zipper of my pants. She pushed both my pants and my boxer briefs down over my hips. Alex's fantasy ended the moment my pants hit the floor. The arsehole in me pushed Alex back down until she was flat against the desk. I kicked out of my favourite boots and socks and stepped out of my pants and briefs. In all my naked glory I moved closer to Alex.

'Huh,' and a frustrated tsk left Alex's mouth. She was cute mad. She could fuck her frustration out on me. I would let her, too. She needed more than one release to mellow her out from her earlier shitty attitude. I knew she would feel good after she came, and it may even make her orgasm amazing.

I stroked myself and let go as I leant over her, letting my hardness brush against her sex as I whispered close to her ear, 'Are you ready?'

Alex just shook her head. 'Protection?'

'There will be no one else but you, Alex.'

'Does that mean you love me?' Only Alex would be brave enough in this moment to ask that. Stunned I didn't say anything. I couldn't remember if I had told her yet. Maybe not if she had to ask me. Did I love Alex? Of course I did. I just couldn't say those words to her yet.

Would my silence kill this moment? It didn't because Alex's hands reached for my face. She kissed me. I pushed my hardness inside her. I sank myself all the way home. Alex wrapped her legs around me as I pulsed inside of her. I felt the electricity run through me like a wake-up call. I moved my hands from my sides to Alex's body, then brushed her hair back, kissed her hard, and pulled my lips back from hers and pumped my hips.

I moved in and out of Alex at different speeds and I watched her as she enjoyed the feel of me inside of her. I slowed my movements to undo the buttons of her blue shirt to find under her shirt was my favourite black camisole. Under the camisole was, as I hoped it would be, the matching black lacy bra. I almost came.

Did Alex know what she did to me? Was it the same for her? Did we have the same effect on one another? I wanted to believe I was right when I felt Alex's sex muscles tighten around me. A sign was she close, so to help her along I moved my hand down to her clit to rub circles with my thumb.

'Brad,' came out hoarsely from Alex's mouth and that was all I needed to unload my seed in Alex.

A grunt left my mouth as my body shook with its own release. It was a feeling I never wanted to get used to. I wanted every release to feel this good. For me and for Alex.

She unwrapped her legs from around my waist, her sex muscles easing their spasms. I counted five slow breaths and pulled out of Alex. She had started to move to sit up but my hand pushed her back down again. I pushed her thighs back, and Alex moved up the desk, now only her lower legs hung from the edge.

I re-dressed myself as Alex watched me. I loved the feel of her eyes on me. She watched as I pulled on the last thing she stripped off. I continued in the order she stripped me out of. The tie that hung around my neck, I had another use for it. I could tell by the look on her face that she enjoyed every minute of my re-dress.

Alex sat up. I didn't bother to push her back down this time as the show was over. I pulled on my socks and boots. It was my turn to watch as Alex got dressed. Her legs automatically crossed when she sat up to stop me leaking out of her.

'Oh my,' fell out of Alex's mouth, and the thought that there would be some of us left behind when I picked Alex up from the desk crossed my mind. When she finished buttoning up her shirt, she wiggled on the spot and brushed her skirt smooth from under her legs.

Time to take this woman inside her dream house. I pulled my tie from my neck and position it over Alex's eyes and tied it behind her head. I picked her up, one arm under her legs, the other behind her back.

'What about the desk?' she asked as I moved us towards the door and unlocked it. 'Our mess?'

'I'll clean it up later, baby cakes.'

Twenty-eight

'I'll clean it up later, baby cakes,' Brad told me as I was carried away from the space we'd just had sex in. The space I would have turned into my office, if the space was mine, but it wasn't. I couldn't see what Brad was up to and I didn't know what his plan was. All I could do was wonder.

I didn't know where Brad was headed with me in his arms. All I knew was I had been lain down on something soft, and Brad had now covered me with his body. Even fully clothed in this suit he felt amazing against me. He moved his body to just beside me, rather than give me his full weight. I was helplessly trapped underneath one of his arms and one of his legs.

Brad didn't remove my blindfold.

'Talk to me?' Brad whispered like we were caught in the eye of a cyclone, like somehow in this moment, he knew there was a storm headed our way. 'You've been cranky since the moment we got here.'

'I can't afford to be pulled away from work just because you demand it.' I huffed out before I added, 'I quit my full-time job. My accounting business is my only income until I get Top Shelf Financial Planning up and running.

'I know,' Brad replied calmly. But what was it that he thought he knew? Because I was damned if I did.

'How?' I asked, a slight irritation in my voice. How did Brad know what I had been up to? I hadn't told him what my plan was even when we sat next to each other for those two weeks.

'Who do you think ordered your business cards and magnets for Alex Black Accounting?'

'You did that? I wanted to run fresh eyes over the design before I hit purchase.'

'Your design is amazing. I gave it the once-over for you.' Did Brad think that if I couldn't see him, I wouldn't be as angry? He would be wrong. 'Your cards, magnets and surprise arrived today.'

'I didn't see them.' Nothing had been delivered to me, and I had been at home all morning.

'That's because I brought them with me. They're in the boot of my car,' Brad confessed.

'You drove three hours for a delivery?' I asked, a little curious as to what Brad's answer would be.

'I drove three hours in a suit just to see you, baby cakes.' Then he whispered, 'It was an uncomfortable three hours.'

'You say that like you missed me,' I joked.

'Every day, for the last two weeks I missed you,' Brad told me light-heartedly, and I smiled at the words I heard him say.

Every night for two weeks I'd dreamt about Brad and wished that he would walk back into my life and here he was. I guess I wanted to know if he loved me as much as I loved him. I felt tears sting my eyes, and I wanted to take this damn blindfold off. I moved my hand to push Brad's tie away and wipe my eyes, but Brad's fingers entwined with mine and stopped me.

'I was getting used to throwing myself into my work so I didn't have to think about you or wait for you to show up.' I felt Brad press his lips into my fingertips then my forehead. I was here because Brad brought me here. I guess I had to wait to see how the rest of my day would unfold.

When I couldn't take the silence any longer, I wriggled out of the hold Brad had on me. I slipped off the blindfold as I sat up.

'Tell me you're not ready to quit?' Those words out of Brad's mouth shocked me. This moment was a push to be together rather than being pulled apart.

I couldn't speak. How did Brad know about the lyrics I'd sung last night? I watched as Brad pulled his phone out from his pocket and pressed play on a video he had been sent.

'I ain't ready to quit.' Brad let those words hang between us. 'Please don't give up on me,' were the next words Brad spoke as I wiped away the tears I had started to cry.

'Never,' I whispered my reply as I moved off the bed and took a couple of steps towards the bedroom door.

'Please don't leave,' Brad pleaded with me.

Could I really leave this man? I reached the threshold of the bedroom and the rest of the house. But somehow, I just couldn't seem to step over it.

'Is this the moment everything changes?' I whispered the question to myself as I leaned up against the door frame.

'Hmm,' he breathed out just above my ear.

I turned around to find he had moved off the bed and had come to stand behind me. He was so close my hands landed on his chest and his arms automatically wrapped around my waist. My touch on his chest, his squeeze of my waist lit a spark between us. 'I don't know what we are,' almost slipped from my mouth. But I bit my lip and held my words in my mouth.

'Come on, let me show you around.' Brad let me go and walked past me.

But I didn't follow him. I was stuck at the threshold of this bedroom.

'Baby cakes,' Brad said as he took my hand and pulled me over the threshold.

He pulled me out the house the same way he carried me in, and I didn't get to see any of the house. Brad unlocked his car and handed over a business card and a magnet from the boxes on his back seat. I busied myself as I gave them both a once over. What I held in my hands was my own creation.

Amazing! Just like Brad said.

He disappeared around the back of his car like he was up to something. He had given me a business card and magnet to distract me. When I finished looking at them, I saw Brad had staked a sign in front of the office space that was attached to this property – one of the reasons I'd wanted to purchase this property for myself.

The staked sign was an exact copy of the front of the business card I held in my hand. 'What is that?' I fumed at Brad.

'Your surprise,' Brad replied as I debated with myself if I really needed a sign.

'Why would you put that there?' As soon as the words left my mouth, Brad had come up to me. His hand landed on my shoulder, and his thumb rubbed circles on my neck.

'The sign is yours, so is this office and the house if you really don't want me to live in it with you.'

What did he just say! Did Brad really just purchase this property to give it away to me. I wanted to ask 'why' but I couldn't get my voice to work. I was having trouble accepting what this man was offering. I was the independent one trying to prove I could do this all myself.

My hands covered my face as tears welled in my eyes and rolled down my face. My body shook with sobs. I didn't know what was happening to me, but as Brad picked me up again and carried me back inside, I had begun to realise what he'd been trying to tell me.

This was Brad telling me he wasn't walking away. Those stakes in the ground told me that was Brad staking his future right here, right now and if I would only stop fighting with him, I would see he was staking his claim on me. He had bought my dream house as a peace offering. A way to help me out now that I had two businesses.

We hadn't got to that part yet, but I knew he loved me. I just wanted him to say that he did. Brad hadn't told me, and I didn't blame him. I had been horrible to him from the moment he had dragged me away from my makeshift office that was my kitchen table.

Brad lay me down on the bed that I wondered would be ours one day, if that was how I understood what he was telling me. I curled myself into a ball and cried. Worse than when my attack played on repeat, my shitty attitude was stuck on a loop I couldn't escape from. I cried harder at what an idiot I was.

Brad lay down behind me, wrapped me up in his arms and let me cry until there was nothing left. Exhausted, I fell asleep.

Twenty-nine

Lex

I had cried myself to sleep. When I woke up, I was surrounded by darkness. I didn't know what time it was, and I didn't care. What I did care about was that I was wrapped up in the arms of a man who made me feel things I didn't know were possible.

Was what we had love? Or the start of it? I wasn't sure and we hadn't spoken about it. Hadn't told each other those words. What I did know was that this relationship wasn't over because of my crankiness or shitty behaviour earlier.

Rolling over, I lay with my nose almost touching Brad's. His arms were around me. He was still here. He hadn't left and I felt no need to ruin this moment by walking out or pushing this man away. I never wanted to be apart from him.

I wasn't sure if Brad was asleep or not, but I knew I had disturbed him when I moved. I spoke into the stillness around me.

The darkness and my sleepiness made me braver than normal. I used it to ask questions I wanted the answers to.

'You're still here?' I whispered, too afraid to touch this man in case he vanished into a puff of thin air.

'I have nowhere else to be, Alex.' The gravel in Brad's sleep-hazed voice caused a wetness to pool in my sex. I wanted this man, but I needed to talk to him more.

'What about your job? Your apartment?' I asked as I poked Brad's chest more than once with my pointer finger, just to check he really was still here. Why did he have nowhere else to be?

'I quit, and the apartment was never mine.' Brad hadn't opened his eyes but he knew where my fingers were, and he entwined them with his. Then he brought our hands up to kiss my palm before Brad rested my hand on his cheek.

'You quit?' His answer surprised me, and I couldn't help but question him as to why he would want to do that.

'When I left you at Zach's to return to Melbourne it almost killed me to walk away as all I wanted to do was comfort you. I didn't want to leave but my father demanded my presence for a new case.'

'Oh,' I breathed out, as Brad breathed in.

He had taken a moment before he explained. 'I knew from the morning I left you in my apartment alone that if I kept working for my dad, he would have driven a wedge between us.'

'You quit everything you have ever known because of me?' If the answer was yes, how was I meant to feel about this man?

'Yes,' Brad whispered as he opened his eyes to look at me. Maybe he needed to check if I was about to bolt. When my hand didn't leave his face, Brad gave me his sweet smirk. I watched as one side of his mouth lifted, so sexy, I wanted to kiss him breathless. But I didn't. I moved only my mouth. There was still too much I wanted to know.

'Why?' I had never known anyone to do that. Everything that had happened between us since my attack was all new. No man had ever or would ever make me feel the way he did.

'I couldn't stand the thought of being too far away from you,' was Brad's answer. I didn't have a reply, but it didn't matter. Brad spoke again. 'Even when I helped your dad to catch that arsehole Paul Christensen, who you know has been wanted for GBH ever since he assaulted you and almost killed Connor.'

'Is that where you have been since you quit your job?' I asked as my hand left Brad's face in search of his hand.

'For a week after I left you in my apartment, I spent it with your father, the following week and these last two I have been finishing up my case notes.' I kissed his palm and let his hand cup my face. Brad's hand moved down my neck to my shoulder and back again. His touch sent tingles through me, and my body shivered.

'Did you catch him?' I asked then held my breath as Brad answered me.

'It was my idea to keep up the ruse coming and going from your apartment to attract Paul's attention. It worked because he tried a surprise attack on me the night you left Melbourne and I came to leave my things at your apartment. Your father tailed me that night. Paul and I wrestled. Then I heard the sound of metal clanging, and your dad had pulled his handcuffs out behind me. Before I knew it, Paul had been slammed against the ground and handcuffed.'

'My father took him down hard just like he said he would. I hope he rots in the hole they put him in,' I said, letting out the breath I'd held in and moving closer to Brad. Now I needed to feel Brad's lips on mine. I only wanted my lips to meet his, but Brad took over to deepen what I had started. I let him. We rolled over. Brad was now on top of me and pressed his weight into me. I could feel how hard he was pressed against my sex.

I knew where this was headed, but was that what I really wanted? The answer would always be yes. But there was something I needed to do. Something I needed to say first. I moved both of my hands to either side of Brad's face.

'I'm sorry my attitude has been so shitty,' I told Brad as I moved my face to within an inch from his. 'I just can't seem to figure you out, and you never answered my question.'

'You want to figure me out?' Brad asked as we locked eyes, and I nodded my head. 'And what question have you asked that I never answered?'

Well, here went nothing and everything. 'Does that mean you love me?' I whispered out the question I'd asked earlier, then I bit into my lower lip. I wanted to believe I knew what Brad would say. But that didn't mean he didn't know how to surprise me.

'You did ask me that.' I nodded my head as Brad spoke again. 'And I didn't answer, did I?' I shook my head.

There was a silence between us as we stared at each other and gathered our thoughts.

'I knew when I quit my job I couldn't say those words to you.' Brad gave me his honesty.

'Why?' I wanted to know why the man above me hadn't told me how he felt yet.

'Because it didn't seem fair to say them if I couldn't guarantee I would be right here next to you every morning.' I threaded my fingers into his hair when he said, 'Those words have played on repeat in my head for what feels like forever.'

Tell me. Please just tell me. 'What words are those?' I wanted Brad to say them first.

Brad rolled us until we lay on our sides and faced each other. When he moved his hands over my body, I moved my hands to the hem of his tee-shirt. I held on for dear life and waited.

'Does sex with no protection mean that I love you?' Brad had shocked me with his words so much that my hand came up to cover my open mouth. Couldn't he have just said I love you?

'I would hope so, baby cakes.'

What was so hard about saying I love you?

Moving my hand, Brad then leaned in and stole my words before he planted a kiss on my lips. When he pulled his lips away from mine, I heard the sweetest words. 'I love you, Alex Black.'

'Make love to me,' I said. 'I want to feel your whiskers on my skin.'

'Alex,' Brad clipped before he smirked.

'Mr Waters,' I huffed out at Brad for calling me Alex.

He reached for one of my breasts and lay his hand over me.

'Okay, okay,' I said, and before Brad had a chance to pinch my nipple, I whispered, 'I love you too, Brad Waters.'

Brad rolled us again and let me straddle him. He sat up and reached behind him to pull his tee-shirt over his head. A movement I found to be hot but not as hot as when his hard cock rubbed against my wet sex.

My man had made light work of the clothes I still wore. He unzipped my skirt and pulled it over my head, then he moved to the buttons on my shirt and undid them. Brad pushed my shirt over my shoulders and down my arms, the same as I had done to him the last time we were intimate this way.

The feel of his hands on my bare skin made me shiver. My arms automatically went up as Brad pulled my black camisole over my head to reveal the black lacy bra that matched the lacy G-string Brad had already torn off me. My hands as they came back down landed on Brad's shoulders. Before I knew it, my bra was gone and so were Brad's black boxer briefs.

Leaning down to place my lips on Brad's skin, I didn't kiss his lips. I kissed everywhere else, his angled jaw, the side of his neck, his left then his right nipple, before leaving a trail of butterfly kisses down over his abs to his belly button. I kissed the tip of his hard cock then licked his shaft. When I reached the top, I sucked Brad into my mouth. Two pumps of my lips up and down had him pulling my body closer to him. Any moment now and I would be impaled. Rocking my hips, I spread my wetness along Brad's shaft.

We were doing this without the fun of any foreplay because Brad was now inside me, pulsing his cock and rocking his hips back and forth. My sex tightened, and after a few more rocks back and forth, I let go.

Brad pulled me down to kiss me and held onto to me as he pulled out and pushed back into me. We moved together, up and down. Every few pumps of Brad's cock he would pulse inside me, and I would gasp. We moved frantically as we tried to chase our own bliss.

'Lean back,' Brad whispered to me as he stopped kissing me and stilled inside of me.

He pushed my chest away from him until I had to put hands behind me to stop from falling too far back where Brad fell out of me.

When I was where Brad wanted me, one hand went to my hip to hold me in place. Then he took his other hand and pressed his thumb into my bundle of nerves. He rubbed circles over my most sensitive spot, softly at first, then harder the more ragged my breathing became.

'Baby cakes,' I breathed out as I felt my sex muscles tighten around Brad. I used the same endearment Brad called me, and I wondered what those words did to him. My body started to shake and so did Brad's. We came at the same time, and now I was breathless and lost for words.

'Baby cakes,' Brad breathed back.

Brad moved his hands to pull me back towards him. I fell forward and he wrapped his arms around me. 'Those words sounded so good, breathless off of your lips.'

He shared his sexy half grin with me, and I couldn't help but say that endearment again. 'Baby cakes.'

When Brad rolled us over, he fell out of me. He lay on top of me and pulled his lips up into a full smile but didn't speak. He just took his lips and placed them on my body from my mouth to my ear down my neck to breasts where he licked, sucked and bit one of my nipples.

'You're supposed to do that before, not after,' I told Brad with my trademark eyebrow raised.

'Who's to say that sex can't be the foreplay,' Brad said as he matched my raised eyebrow and then gave me in his trademark smirk again. 'If you're complaining, I could just stop.'

I shook my head and put my hands on either side of Brad's face and pushed him back to where I wanted him: my man playing with my nipples. He complied with his mouth on one nipple, before he moved the arm that held himself up and reached his fingers across to pinch my other nipple.

My body bucked, but not from the sting as he played with my nipples. No, my shoulders dug into the bed and my hips lifted into the air when Brad pushed not one but two fingers inside my pussy.

I nearly came as my hips landed back on the bed. Tears welled in my eyes as I wondered how much more my body could take. What Brad was doing now and had already done to my body, I had never done or experienced before. This moment was too much for me.

My previous partners left me feeling like there had to be more. The sex had been vanilla, and it made me wonder if it was me that was boring. But Brad had read my body language, read me so easily, like it wasn't that hard if you just listened. The man above had learnt what I liked and what I didn't, and no one had ever listened to me or my body before.

Brad continued pumping his fingers into me until my body shook and I had come again. Then he kissed my forehead and moved off the bed. I guess this wasn't the right moment to tell Brad about the contraception I'd given up taking when I decided I was climbing the corporate ladder and wasn't looking for a boyfriend or even a one-night stand.

As much as I wanted to get off this bed and go and explore this house I was in, I would need to find some clothes and the shower. But I just couldn't bring myself to move. My legs wouldn't work either. All I could do was roll onto my side and snuggle into this bed and the doona.

Thirty

Brad

I may have gone a little too far when I stuck my fingers inside of Alex to make her come a second time. At least now I knew how far I could take our sexual encounters. If Alex thought I didn't see her eyes water through the emotions she felt, she didn't know me very well at all.

I had seen the wetness in her eyes when I kissed her forehead. I was just glad she didn't follow me off the bed. When I checked on Alex a few minutes later, she had fallen asleep. I kissed her forehead again, but I needed a shower and a change of clothes. Then I had work to do.

Alex's office required my attention. It was time to make her office a space that suited her. The walls needed to be prepped for their first coat of paint. I opened the French doors that led me inside this office, latching the doors to keep them open. Then I moved the desk out onto the veranda.

I covered the floorboards with a drop sheet and went to town on the prep work I needed to do. The walls needed to be washed, then I needed to patch the holes the previous owners hanging pictures made. When I finished my prep work, I went to check on Alex. She was still asleep. Time for me to paint.

As I made my way back to the office, I noticed there was a vehicle in the driveway. I made my way up the steps as my visitor exited their vehicle.

I wasn't expecting anyone. I was new to town and didn't know anyone. How did anyone know to look for me here?

My visitor made his way over to me. He took a look inside the empty space that was the office before he spoke again. 'Name's Brock Michaels, I'm a friend of Harley and Zach's. I'm a builder and you look like you could do with some of my help.'

'Brad Waters.' I stuck my hand out for my visitor to shake, which he did with a solid grip.

'Yeah, thanks to you I was able to purchase the house next door to Zach's,' Brock told me as I remembered the work I had done for The Harley James Trust and The James Family Trust.

'I'm glad it all worked out for you.' I was happy that some of the work I had done for my father worked out for the better.

'Thanks, man. You want me to hang around, give you a hand?'

'I've washed and patched the holes. I just need to give it a paint.'

'Let's get to it,' Brock said as he went to get his paint gear from his work truck.

I needed to get my paint gear from the garage. Brock cut in the roof and architraves while I cut in the skirting boards, door and window frames. The walls and roof were already white. They both just needed a freshen up, one coat of paint would be enough.

'What's the style for the office?' Brock asked as we finished up painting.

'I'm going for black accessories on a white canvas, and not just because Alex's surname is Black. Her business is Top Shelf Financial Planning, and I want this space to be classy,' I replied.

'If you need help with the set-up, let me know, I'll give you a hand,' Brock said as he handed over one of his cards. 'Zach told me Lex does his books. I normally do it myself but with all the work I have on at the moment, I need someone to take over. I thought Lex might like a new client.'

'I'll get Alex to reach out when her office is set up and ready to go,' I told Brock. I hoped Alex was ready to take on new clients.

'Thanks, man,' Brock said as he fist-pumped my closed hand.

'Thanks for your help too.'

After he'd left, I stripped off and waited for the shower to heat up before I got in. I washed myself clean of paint before I let the water cascade over me as I rested my forearms against the wall. I didn't even hear Alex approach. I didn't even know she was behind me until she touched my shoulder with her lips on my skin. I turned around to see her sleepy eyes meet mine.

'Did I wake you?'

Alex just shook her head at my question.

'Everything okay?' I asked. The look on Alex's face told me she was worried about something.

But Alex didn't answer me. She turned her head away from me.

'Alex,' I clipped, but she didn't look at me until she started to speak.

'Why do you always call me that?'

That wasn't what was on Alex's mind, but it was what she asked me. Her question started our conversation, and I had to answer her.

'How many people call you Alex?' I asked, curious. I thought that I knew the answer, but I wanted Alex to tell me.

'Only when I'm in trouble. Everyone calls me Lex, I insist. My parents call me Honeybee.'

There it was. Black and white. No one called her by her Christian name except me. I would always call her Alex, unless I wanted to call her baby cakes. I knew Alex secretly loved it when I called her by her Christian name, as something told me Alex went gooey inside.

I leaned forward, closer to Alex, and just above her ear I said, 'No one calls you your Christian name. That's why I call you Alex. I know somewhere inside you like it when I do.' When I moved away from Alex's ear, I gave her my trademark smirk. But it was gone with the next words that came out of her mouth.

'Did you know I'm not on the pill?' Alex's words were barely audible. My hands reached up to cup each side of her face, and I didn't interrupt what Alex was about to say to me. 'What are the chances of me falling pregnant the first time you and I have unprotected sex?'

'I don't know. Does it worry you?'

By the serious look on Alex's face, she was a little worried.

'I've just started to kick off a new business venture. It's not even off the ground yet. What if I'm pregnant? Am I going to be able to support myself off my accounting business?'

'Baby cakes.' I pressed my lips to Alex's, and when I pulled away, I said, 'I'm not going anywhere, and if we are pregnant, we will make it work. We'll figure something out.'

'I've always been careful. What was I thinking?' Alex gave herself a verbal bashing. I needed to lighten the mood.

'I hope you were thinking that you loved me?' I made eye contact and half smiled when I said my words.

'Brad, I'm serious.' Alex slapped my chest. Thank God she took my words for what they were.

'Alex, I'm here. We have this house. You have your businesses and if you will let me, I would like to help you build it.'

'How?' A little bit of Alex's sass came out. I could see the last twenty-four hours had started to take its toll on her.

'As your business partner.' I threw it out to see how Alex would react.

'I'm listening.' More of her sass. Now that I had her attention, I needed to give my pitch to Alex with everything I had.

'I could do the books while you grow your financial planning business.' I let my words sink in before I said, 'I could study, or you could teach me, but I think we could make it work, baby cakes.'

Alex turned over in her head what I said, then she smiled. 'If we do this, we need more business.' I opened my mouth to say I already had a new business, but Alex hadn't finished what she wanted to say. 'If it all goes to shit though between us, I get the house, the businesses, the baby if I'm pregnant, and you get to leave quietly.'

'Lucky for you, I don't plan on you and me going to shit, plus I already have a new client for you.' I couldn't help myself. I was a keeper, and I needed Alex to see that.

'Guess you and I will need some sort of a contract.'

I loved how smart this woman was; she knew she had to set boundaries when it came to her businesses.

'I know someone who might be able to help with that.'

Alex and I shared smirks. 'Would you feel better if I just asked you to marry me?'

'Oh my God. Are you serious? Please don't ask me now, I'm not ready. I want us to live together longer than two weeks and work together for a couple of months and if we haven't killed each other, then you can ask me.'

Alex was right, we needed to spend some time together under the same roof to see how we melded together. 'Okay, baby cakes, we'll do it your way.'

'I love you,' Alex told me as she pushed me out of the spray of the water to have a shower by herself.

'I love you too,' I told Alex as I left her to turn over our conversation.

'Come on, I'm taking you for dinner.' I was going to have to learn how to cook. There was no way we could afford to eat out every night. If I knew how to cook, I could sate Alex then feed her dinner. We wouldn't have to leave the house. But I would have to wait until the house was ready to be lived in before I did any of that.

'The Grand Hotel?' Alex asked, and a smile played on her lips.

'Is there another pub in town I need to know about?' This town was new to me. I didn't know the layout yet.

Alex's answer was a shake of her head. Good to know.

'I have paperwork I need to take back there. Plus, I need to change out of these clothes.'

'We may as well grab an overnight bag while we're at your house.'

Alex launched herself at me and wrapped her limbs around me. I caught her and because she was in my arms, I kissed her. Probably harder than I needed to. But I couldn't help myself, I was in love with the woman I held onto.

Epilogue

Brad, Six Months Later

Alex wasn't allowed inside the house while I helped my mother weave her magic. I just hoped in the end that Alex would love what my mother and I had come up with. There was a need for a happy medium between Alex's cosiness and my starkness. It had been six months since I'd brought a cranky Alex to see her dream house.

Alex loved what I had done with her office: black accessories on a white background. Her expectations for her house after she saw her office were of a standard I didn't know if I could achieve. Maggie Waters thought otherwise. But I would have to wait until I let Alex see the rest of her house to see if she was happy with the design.

I had convinced Alex to let me work with her. She didn't pay me. I had told her not to. Plus, I had money from when I'd worked with my father that I'd never spent, and there was more than enough left in the account my mother had given me. Even though Alex was still trying to build her businesses to the point where she could make it successful and live off the money she made comfortably. She was the breadwinner of our household, but I was going to offer my services as lawyer if we needed extra money.

Alex and I hadn't killed each other. I thought everything was great, and that we worked well together. We worked side by side while she showed me how to do everything she did. Then at the end of the day I would sit down and work my way through my online training. It hadn't escaped me that Alex also disappeared at the end of her day to work on something she wouldn't show me. Or tell me anything about.

I don't know why but I could tell Alex was still worried. What was the possibility for Alex's stress? I mentally ticked off what I knew: her dream house was paid for, her inner-city apartment was paid for. Her childhood home was almost paid off too. She didn't have an astronomical amount of debt. Alex was good with her money, and her accounting business was okay too. Alex had landed The Grand Hotel account and picked up new business – her brother's friend who ran his own small building business. Alex had only just managed to convince Zach and Connor to be clients for her new business.

I could help her out too, if she needed money. We could come to some agreement if she wanted a partner. But if I knew Alex at all, she wanted to do this on her own terms without anyone's help just to prove that she could do it. And she was getting there. There must be something else that my woman was worried about. And I was about to find out what that something was.

Alex and I had been staying at her childhood home that backed onto the river, while I got our house ready. Alex's house was close to a full house at times. Connor and Morgan had been staying with us while their bungalow was being fitted out.

But today as I pulled up outside of Alex's house, I noticed the black Mercedes in the driveway. One guess: Alex's parents were here.

As I walked through the front door, I found Connor, Morgan, Preston, Eva Black and Alex in some sort of discussion. I didn't know what they were all talking about, I stood just inside the front door and listened. Alex had her back to me. She didn't know I was there.

'Honeybee,' Eva Black said as she stood in front of her daughter and rubbed her arms up and down. 'Have you decided what you will do with this house?'

'No one is suggesting that you put the house on the market or rent the house out, Honeybee,' Preston Black told his daughter.

'Who says I have to do anything with this house?' The moment the words left Alex's mouth, I could tell her family had made her cranky.

'The house will be empty,' Connor stated, 'when you move in with Brad. Do you really want strangers here? I know you bought this house for a reason.'

'I did. This house will always be an open door for this family. I'm not giving that up and if that means this house will be empty, I'm okay with that. I want to keep this house in our family.'

'Honeybee, both Harley and Morgan are pregnant. Harley is due any day now. Your father and I would like to be closer now that we have grandbabies on the way,' Eva Black added, then said. 'We could be here for you when you decide to have your family. Would you consider selling your house back to us.'

'I'm not selling,' Alex was adamant with her words.

'Now that Paul has been sentenced to fourteen years in prison, it's time to retire and spend some time with my grand-babies. Please think about selling. Or at least think about letting us stay here.'

Who would have thought Preston Black would retire for his grandbabies? As for Paul, he got what he deserved.

'Okay I'll think about it. Thanks for the update on Paul, Dad.' Alex whispered, then she turned to face me when she heard me speak.

'I'm going to steal Alex away. I have a surprise for her.' I reached out my hand for her as she walked towards me.

Out the corner of my eye I saw Alex's hand as it covered her mouth when she realised where we were headed. But I didn't let Alex get out of my car as I parked it in the garage of the house I had bought for her. I saw her hand reach for the handle.

Alex turned to face me, the same now as when we had pulled up to her brother's house in her suped-up black Commodore over seven months ago. I didn't kiss Alex that day when I knew I wanted to, and only our foreheads and noses had touched. Today when I reached out to cup Alex's face and pull her closer to me, I knew my lips would touch hers.

When my lips pressed into Alex's, I held her to me for a moment before I let her go. 'This moment with my lips on yours is what I wanted the moment I pulled up at your brother's house.'

I unlocked the doors and got out. I made my way to the door that would lead me inside.

'Wait,' Alex said as she stepped out of my car. 'If you have brought me here, does that mean the house is ready and I get to see it?'

I nodded my head and watched as Alex made her way over to me. She kissed my cheek then took off into the house to look around.

I leant up against the door frame of the internal garage door as Alex screamed her Oh my Gods over every inch of her house. When she came to a standstill in the living room, I walked up behind her and wrapped my arms around her.

'I take it you like the way the house is styled?' I asked close to Alex's ear.

Alex shook her head before she whispered, 'I don't just like it, I love it'.

'Move in with me?' I pressed my lips into her neck and nibbled on her skin. Alex squirmed before she turned around in my arms and looked into my eyes.

'I've waited six months for you to say those words to me. Yes.' Alex kissed my lips then, pressed her lips to mine and went in search of my tongue. Before our kiss ended up out of control, I pulled away.

'You want to tell me what's going on, Alex?' I asked, then waited for her to respond.

'My parents want me to sell them my house, but I don't think I can.' She told me, but there was more.

'You don't have to decide right now. Let them split their time between here and Melbourne, the same as you have done.' I stood back from Alex. 'We're a team, baby cakes, always, but I can't help you if you won't tell me anything. What else is going on?'

Alex took a deep breath, then said. 'I've always been interested in personal finance so I signed myself up for the financial advisor's course. I'm almost qualified.'

'I wondered what you were up to while I was studying,' I said as I watched Alex's eyebrow's knit together.

'Well, I've been working on plans for Connor's and Zach's money in hope that I can kick off Top Shelf Financial Planning. I want to help all my family and friends with their finances, but I don't know if they'll pay me for it. As much as I want my new idea to take off, I won't be able to commit to more work once the baby is due.'

Baby. A baby, I repeated over and over in my head. Alex and I hadn't even been trying. We decided we needed to use protection. Contraception for her and condoms for me. With the adventures we had recently embarked on, we told ourselves we were being sensible.

But the universe had other plans. A pill missed here, and a condom missed there. But Alex and I loved each other, and we told each other we would be okay. So, perhaps we weren't that sensible.

Alex's news came as a surprise. We hadn't killed each other. We had melded together in such a way that we were going to have a baby. When Alex told me about our baby, I knew I wouldn't be able to live without her now.

I pulled Alex onto my lap, and we rocked back and forth as I whispered, 'It's okay, it's going to be okay,' as my thumbs rubbed circles on her neck.

'Baby cakes, we will figure it out. You can take as much or as little maternity leave as you need, then you can build up Top Shelf Financial Planning.' I kissed Alex's forehead, let her absorb my words.

Alex sniffled as she listened to me. I leaned my forehead into the side of Alex's face and breathed in the scent of her skin before I said, 'Alex, your businesses will be okay, our baby will be okay, and you and I will be okay.' I stopped for a breath, before I whispered, 'You may have to marry me now though.'

'If you're asking me right now, you better have my ring.' The little bit of sass that Alex liked to use on me came out.

'Baby cakes, I'm not down on one knee and I haven't even asked your parents.' I smirked at Alex. A tip upwards of one side of my lip, the one I knew sent my woman crazy. 'And I'm going to wait until you look so damn sexy to ask you to marry me. Your black lace drives me crazy.' I now had to figure out a creative way to ask Alex to marry me. I did owe Alex more than one lacy black G-string. Maybe I could purchase her new lingerie, sexy black lace lingerie, and get her to try it on for me, then I could drop to one knee and pop the question.

I reached down to press play on Dierks Bentley's 'Black'. The song he wrote about his wife, her maiden name Black the same as Alex's.

'I love it,' Alex said of the song as she moved to straddle me. She cupped my face and pressed her lips to mine. Alex bit me, then swiped her tongue across my bottom lip before she continued to kiss me harder. It was game on when I picked Alex up and lay her down on our lounge. I pressed my body into Alex's and never once did we break our kiss. I needed to make love to my woman, christen our house and fill it with all our love now that we had a baby on the way. I was one happy man.

ACKNOWLEDGEMENTS

Thank you to my editor and publisher Dr Juliette Lachemeier at The Erudite Pen, who inspired the honing of my writing craft. I know the edges of book three aren't as rough. To my book cover designer Judith San Nicolas for taking the ideas I have thrown into the mixing pot to come out with a totally drool-worthy cover – your work is amazing. To my wonderful family and husband Craig – you are still encouraging me to pursue my writing dreams. To my mum Susan for being my sounding board and the person who reads the messy first drafts. To my ARC readers, thank you for being brave enough to read the words I have written. Your insight is invaluable and your support is truly appreciated as I work on making The Acoustic Make You Mine Romance Series a reality.

ABOUT THE AUTHOR

Kimberley Anne was born and raised on the border of New South Wales and Victoria. The small country town she grew up in is the inspiration for the fictional town in her novel. Kimberley completed her Bachelor of Arts in 2001 where she majored Professional Writing at Victoria University, Melbourne. She began writing her debut novel in 2018 after her husband gifted her a Kindle.

With life experience on her side, Kimberley moved on from her country-town beginnings and is now based in Brisbane, Australia. When Kimberley isn't looking for her next book idea or having her nose in her Kindle, she can be found kicking back with a margarita in her hand and her German Shepherds at her feet.

Black Lace is Kimberley's third book in the Make You Mine Romance novels, Acoustic Series, where she blends romance with real-life challenges, music, passion and plenty of heat. Her first two novels in the series *Blackout* and *Black Eye* were met with rave reviews and flew off the shelves.

Black Out

A Make You Mine Romance

KIMBERLEY ANNE

Book One is available at all major booksellers

Book Two is available at all major booksellers

What's next for Kimberley Anne's readers?

The Make You Mine world is far from over...

Book 4 dives back into Harley and Zach's turbulent love story, this time through Zach's eyes. Will his side of the story change everything you thought you knew?

Book 5 turns the spotlight on Brock and Shea (from Books 1 and 3). Sparks fly as they find their way to each other, but small-town drama and the ever-present Black siblings may make or break them.

Book 6 follows Jaime and Ella, Jackie's son and Lex's friend from Book 2, as they discover love and family in the wake of heartbreak.

And that's not all... Kimberley is also working on a 30,000-word standalone novella that's already in the final stages. Short, sharp, and full of all the passion and emotion you crave, this one's going to be spicy.

Stay tuned. The next chapter is closer than you think...

Enjoyed the book? You can follow the author at:

Website: www.kimberleyanneauthor.com

Email: info@kimberleyanneauthor.com

FB: https://www.facebook.com/authorkimberleyanne

Instagram: www.instagram.com/kimberleyanneauthor/

If you liked the book, please leave a review on Amazon, Goodreads or with the author directly. Reviews are invaluable in supporting an author's hard work and are greatly appreciated.